CONGRESS PARK SCHOOL
District 102
Brookfield, Il.

Junebug in Trouble

Junebug
in Trouble

ALICE MEAD

Farrar Straus Giroux
New York

Library of Congress Cataloging-in-Publication Data
Mead, Alice.
    Junebug in trouble / Alice Mead.— 1st ed.
        p.   cm.
    Sequel to: Junebug and the Reverend.
    Summary: Despite having moved out of the rough housing
project where he grew up, ten-year-old Junebug continues to
encounter crime, gangs, and violence.
    ISBN 0-374-33969-4
    [1. Juvenile delinquency—Fiction.   2. Gangs—Fiction.
3. Single-parent families—Fiction.   4. African Americans—Fiction.]
I. Title.

PZ7.M47887 Jv 2002
[Fic]—dc21

                                                        2001033268

Junebug in Trouble

One

Early in the morning—well, not too early—Reverend Ashford and I are walking along Bellmore Avenue on our way back from the corner store, where we bought a newspaper and two Tootsie Roll pops. We used to buy his cigarettes there, too, but he quit smoking and now he wears a nicotine patch on his arm.

"Guess what. I'll be starting fifth grade next week," I tell him.

"Fifth grade. Hmm. Can't say I remember it at all," he says.

It's the Friday before Labor Day weekend, and Mama has the day off. My mom is the resident supervisor at a home for some elderly people who need medical help. We all live together in a group of little apartments. She doesn't get too many days off, the way I see it.

The weather today is beautiful, with puffy white

clouds and a little breeze to keep things cool. The breeze is tugging at my T-shirt.

"You want to come to the beach with us?" I ask as we turn onto Robin Lane.

"The beach?" Reverend Ashford stops walking and glares at me. "Nope. Too hot," he mutters. "Way too hot."

He always says that. Too hot. Reverend Ashford has emphysema. He likes to sit in his La-Z-Boy recliner and watch game shows while the fan blows on his head. But my mom wants him doing activities. She's the one who made us start taking walks together.

Reverend Ashford and I sit on the bench in the small grassy area at the end of Robin Lane. In June, I planted a little maple tree here, the size of a tall twig. I've been watering it like crazy, but it's taking its time growing.

Reverend Ashford takes the classifieds and folds me a hat, then makes one for himself. We put on the hats and chew our lollipops.

With that breeze, today would be a perfect boat-yard day. Great for sailing. I worked at the Fair Haven boatyard all summer, but my friend Ron down there doesn't want me hanging around in September. That's the time everyone is trying to get his boat hauled in and set up on big sawhorses for the winter. I guess Ron's afraid I might get bonked on the head by a boat. Or maybe he knows I don't want to scrape barnacles every weekend.

Mama's best friend, Harriet, will be driving us to the beach. Harriet lives at the Auburn Street projects, the place we used to live, the place Mama won't let me even visit anymore.

Harriet will be here any minute, but Mama's still rushing around getting ready. Why does it always take my family an hour to get out of the house? I like to do things fast. I check Reverend Ashford's gold pocket watch. It's already nine-thirty. I want to get going now. My buddy Robert's going to be at the beach today, and I can't wait to see him!

I don't have to look in the house to know what Mama's doing. She's shoving everything in the world into our beach bag—towels, flip-flops, sunglasses, radio, lunch, and two packs of chocolate cupcakes, one pack for me and Tasha and one for Robert. The cupcakes are his favorite kind, with creamy goop inside. Robert's got a cupcake thing.

"My mother sure is slow." I sigh.

"She may be slow, but she's one determined woman. She knows how to get her way."

He's talking about how Mama makes him get out and about—the library, a baseball game, picnics, walks with me. She is pretty bossy, with me, too. She wouldn't let me visit Robert once all summer. Not once! She thinks I might get caught in the middle of some fight or shooting or drug deal. I don't know.

Mama wants me to make friends here. But the only kid nearby is Brandon, and he went to live with his grandmother for a while because his mom's in the hospital. Anyway, I won't ever forget about Robert. She shouldn't be choosing my friends for me. That's not right. I feel as if she doesn't trust me or something.

Reverend Ashford opens the sports page and checks for news of the NBA. He's looking for players' sports contracts. He wants to complain about their enormous salaries.

My six-year-old sister, Tasha, has come outside to wait. She's got headphones on and is wearing a lime-green bathing suit. She's bopping around barefoot on the grass as if she doesn't have a care in the world, singing some hip-hop song at the top of her lungs. I bet she's been watching MTV. I thought she wanted to be a ballerina. Ballerinas usually dance to weepy old violin music.

Wait a minute! Is she using my Walkman? How did that happen? Well, I guess I can let her borrow it, at least for a few minutes. "Yo! Tasha! Ask next time," I holler.

She points to the earphones to show me she can't hear me. She's probably got the volume on blasting. I run over, pull one earphone off, and lean forward.

"Ask me next time!" I shout.

"Okay! You got it!"

She dances away, jerking her shoulders and doing hand moves with her index and pinky fingers pointed out like a rap artist.

When did she get like this? I swear she's taller, too. Her legs are longer, and her two front teeth are coming in fast, even compared to the other day. She looks sort of normal for a change. I glare at her and shake my head.

Boy, I can't wait to see Robert again. It's been months since we got together. And that whole time, I've been hanging around Tasha for company. Or Reverend Ashford. I mean, I like him, but he is an old guy who needs oxygen.

I go to the door to try and hurry things up. "Mama!" I yell, peering through the screen door. "Did you remember your driver's license?"

"Oh, shoot," she says, and disappears into her bedroom. Harriet thought today would be a good chance for Mama to practice her driving.

Finally Harriet's old green Hornet turns the corner and pulls up in front of our sidewalk. She gets out, and right away she looks at me with a very strange expression on her face.

Huh? I wonder what's up. Something's going on, that's for sure, and it's about to set me off on an asking frenzy. I am always curious, to the point of driving people crazy with my questions. I go after answers like a noisy, stubborn junebug. I am also a junior—Reeve McClain, Jr. So my nickname Junebug is stuck to me like glue.

"What happened, Harriet? Why are you looking at me funny?"

"I have a secret. A huge secret. And don't even try to guess it, Junebug, because you never will. You'll find out in due time."

Harriet's grinning. I glance at Mama to see if she knows anything about this, but she shrugs as if to say, Don't ask me.

Oh, man. I truly hate secrets. When I don't know something, it bothers me nonstop.

Harriet pats the top of my head. "Sorry, Junebug. You'll have to wait on this one," she says.

"Wait? Till when? Next year? Next century?"

"No. Late this afternoon, maybe."

Hmmm. Afternoon. That's a clue. Maybe she made a cake. Or a batch of brownies.

"Is it a cake? Hey, Harriet, is the secret a chocolate cake?"

"Oh, Lord," my mother says. "Don't let him start."

"You can tell me, Harriet. Is it a cake?"

"No. It is not a cake. Now, don't ask me any more. And don't make your mama nervous while she's learning to drive."

Like a chauffeur, Harriet stands by the car door and helps my mother into the driver's seat. Tasha's standing behind me with a doubtful look on her face.

Mama hardly ever drives, which is no wonder considering we don't have a car.

"Are you sure Mama can drive okay on the highway?" Tasha asks Harriet.

"Of course she can. She'll do just fine."

We pile into the backseat. Tasha's got Theo, her favorite teddy bear, with her. Right away, she unzips a plastic bag full of doll stuff and starts putting a girl doll's bathing suit on him. Poor Theo.

I sit directly behind Mama so I can help navigate. I crane my neck around to look out the back window. "All right. Go ahead. No one's behind us," I call out.

Mama keeps looking in her mirrors.

"Go ahead now. Back right on out. You're doing great."

I am pleased to notice that I sound just like Ron, who's been teaching me to sail.

"Junior, will you please hush up," Mama says, slowly backing into the street. "I've got this made in the shade."

But she must have turned the wheels too soon. The front tire hits the curb, and we lurch over it. Kerthud.

"Oops!" Tasha and I yelp.

Harriet turns around. "That's enough, you two! Now, I mean it. No backseat drivers."

Once we finally get going, Mama drives better, except when she's making turns. Then she drives as slow as a turtle. People behind us honk like mad because they want to get through the lights before they turn red. If I had a horn, I'd honk it right along with them. I want to get to the beach so I can play in the waves with Robert. Just me and Robert all day long.

Two

On the phone last night, Robert told me that the city's recreation department would send two school buses to pick up kids and give them a ride to the beach. Probably a lot of kids from Auburn Street will be at the beach today. Fine with me, as long as they don't interfere with me and my buddy. We have some major catching up to do.

When we get to the beach parking lot, I spot the buses right away. I bet they got here hours ago. We unpack the trunk of the Hornet, and Harriet puts on her great big straw hat with a yellow sunflower on it. Then she leads the way as we head down the board-walk to the beach.

The sun is warm, but not too hot. The tall, dry beach grass on either side of us has a soft, sweet smell and tickles my bare legs as I walk by. The soles of my feet squeak, squeak, squeak in the dry sand.

Once we pass through the dunes, Harriet starts to

11

scout around for the perfect spot to sit. Mama sets our bags down and waits, but I follow Harriet around, trying to figure out exactly what she's doing.

"What difference does it make where we sit? It's all sand, isn't it? Or is that secret you were talking about buried here someplace?" I ask. "Are you a pirate? Maybe you're some kind of pirate."

"What did I tell you? Forget about that secret for now. I have to find the right spot. I'm a professional beachgoer. I can't sit just anywhere."

So I trail after her while she snoops around in search of the perfect location. Dead seaweed is dead seaweed. Sand is sand. What's the big deal? Robert is waiting.

Finally Harriet finds a place she likes. Looks like plain old sand to me. Mama and I glance at each other and laugh. We're both thinking the same thing.

"What?" says Harriet. "You don't like this spot? What's wrong with it?"

"No, no. It's fine. Really!" Mama says.

"Sure is!" I chime in. Mama and I laugh.

"Pfffft! You two don't know how lucky you are to have me around."

Tasha is already spreading out her towel for Theo. I don't know if Theo has been to the beach before. I hope his fur doesn't get all sandy.

Harriet sits down on her neatly spread-out towel. She takes out a big plastic bottle of coconut-smelling oil and rubs it all over her arms and legs. The smell makes me sneeze. Then she smooths the corners of her huge beach towel again and puts rocks in each corner to hold it down. In her bag is a stack of magazines and a big, fat paperback. She plops these down on the towel, too. "There!" she says.

Now Tasha unloads a plastic bucket and shovel and gets to work, digging. "Junebug, you want to dig a tunnel with me?"

"No. I gotta go find Robert."

"The kids seem to be over there, Junebug, by the lifeguard chairs," Mama says, shading her eyes with her hand and squinting. "You make sure you stay in the protected area, Junebug. Do you hear me?"

"Yeah."

I yank my T-shirt over my head and take off down the beach. Robert sees me and comes running over. He leads me to where the other kids are, in front of the lifeguards. Most of them are standing ankle-deep in the water, watching as the waves come in fast and tall, with a lot of tumbling white foam rushing over the sand and swirling around their legs.

"Wow! Look at those waves!" I yell.

"Yeah. We just got here, a few minutes before you. Think we can body-surf in this?" Robert asks. "It's kind of rough." That was our plan, body-surfing.

"The waves are pretty big," I answer. "But who cares! Come on."

Robert doesn't move. "Nobody's going in. Maybe there are jellyfish."

"Afraid of 'em?" I tease.

"No."

I'm not. Jellyfish, smellyfish. I don't care. "Come on! Let's go!"

I back up and then run full speed for the water, leap over the foam, crash through the broken waves, and throw myself at the next full wave with a loud yell.

Under I go, my ears filling with cool water, and I come up for air like a seal. I wish I had flippers. I turn over on my back and float out deeper. I can feel the tug of the next big wave pull me out toward itself as it gathers into a mountain of water. Without any effort at all, I float up and over the top as the crest goes hissing by, leaving a soft spray in the air like tiny soda bubbles. That was so easy!

I love this! I like feeling that the ocean is big and powerful, and I'm safe and sound in my own little body-boat, riding the waves.

There's only one tiny thing wrong. Instead of leaping and diving into the water right along with me, Robert is still standing near the shore, now talking to Trevor and Angelique, a sixth-grader.

Angelique looks beautiful today. She's wearing a long white T-shirt over her bathing suit. I want her to know I'm here, but I'm afraid to say hi.

And Trevor? He's going into seventh. I really can't stand that kid. He tricked me once back in Auburn Street. He and my Aunt Jolita teamed up and tried to get me to squeal on my buddy Darnell. They wanted me to tell a drug dealer where Darnell was when he had run away. The dealer paid them money, too. But I don't want to think about that stuff. That's exactly why my mom decided to move out of there. So I wouldn't have to live with that every day and end up getting sucked into it the way my dad did. Darnell never did come back. I miss him, too, not just Robert.

"Hey!" I put my feet down, and I'm surprised to find that when I stand, with the waves calm now, I'm in only as deep as my waist.

"Hey, Robert! Come on," I yell. "Look! It's not deep here."

He wades in a little farther, gives a shiver, and hugs his skinny arms against his bony-ribbed self. I back up and then flop down as the water breaks all around me. I let the next wave carry me in to their feet and stand up. Angelique smiles at me.

"The water's great!" I say. "Come on, Robert. Come on, Angelique."

Trevor narrows his eyes and looks at me, trying to act fifteen. But he's not. He's going on thirteen. He stayed back once for missing so many days of school.

"Hey, Junebug. How ya doing?" he says.

"I'm doin' all right."

We don't have much to say to each other, that's for sure.

Robert and Angelique run past us and dive into

15

the water. Then they let a wave carry them in, and they get up, dripping and laughing. Angelique pulls a strand of brown seaweed off her shoulder.

"Whoa. A big one's coming!" Angelique points to it. "See it? Come on, Trevor! It's fun."

But I'm watching Trevor's face as he watches the waves, and suddenly I realize he's afraid of the water! That's why he doesn't go in. Maybe he doesn't know how to swim well. The first time I went in the sailboat with Ron, I was heart-thumping scared. But I got over it.

"It's okay being scared of the waves, Trevor. But just kind of go with it. Don't fight the waves, and you'll float right up and over the top," I say.

He turns on me angrily. "Shut up, Junebug. I'm not scared, you jerk. Come on," he says to Angelique, and tries to take her hand. But she twists her wrist, and her long fingers slide out of his grasp. "Come on, I said."

"No. I want to stay with them," Angelique says.

In disgust, Trevor wades out of the water and heads off down the beach. We stand there for a minute, watching him go. Angelique doesn't move. Meanwhile, the undertow is gradually sinking my feet into the sand. I look down to see that I have only ankles; my feet are buried. I didn't mean to make Trevor so upset.

"Junebug, you crazy idiot. Why did you do that?" Robert says. "Now he's angry."

"I didn't do anything. Why does he have to get so mad?"

"Because you told everybody he was scared. Trevor's not scared of anything. You embarrassed him, and he doesn't take disrespect from anybody. Chase after him, Junebug. Tell him you're sorry."

"Sorry? Sorry for what?" I say. "What do you care, anyway? I thought you and I were best friends. I thought you were going to hang out with me today, Robert. So what do you care if he gets angry?"

Robert and I stand in the foamy undertow, staring at each other. I feel confused. I don't understand why this is happening. Why is Robert bothering with Trevor at all? I thought we were going to spend the day together, just the two of us. Why is he making this into a choosing thing, like choosing up sides?

Angelique is watching us.

"Tell him you're sorry, Junebug. Come on. Please?" Robert begs. "I can't have Trevor mad at me."

"No! Cause I'm not sorry. It's not disrespectful to tell someone how to swim in the waves. I was trying to help him out."

Robert turns to Angelique. "You better go with Trevor, then," he says. "Tell him Junebug didn't mean it."

Don't, I want to say, but I hold it inside. Why should everybody have to do whatever Trevor wants? What is this?

Angelique turns around and wades out of the water. Instead of heading up the beach, though, she sits down with her knees drawn up, pushing dark wet sand into a little mound beside her and then smoothing it over with her hand.

I'm frowning. I can feel my face crunched down like Tasha's when she gets mad. I'm supposed to make guys like Trevor happy? Well, too bad! I'm not doing it!

But what if it means Robert and I won't be friends anymore? I swore I would help him forever and ever, that we'd be like brothers.

The waves wash in and out. The two of us stand there for I don't know how long. He's gotta choose me, gotta calm down and stay here with me. But he doesn't.

"I'm going after him," he says finally. "And I'm going to tell him you said you were sorry."

I shrug. "Yeah. Okay," I say. "Whatever."

What the heck. I don't care. But I do care. It's the worst thing in the world if Robert chooses Trevor over me. My cheeks and ears feel hot. Angry tears sting my eyes, making everything blurry. I wade out of the water and sit down. I splash a handful of water on my face to hide my tears. Robert's running off down the beach now. My best friend is running after that creep Trevor.

Now the waves aren't fun. They're noisy and cold. I pull a big strand of flat seaweed off my foot. I want to talk to Angelique, but I don't know what to say. Luckily for me, Angelique speaks first.

"I might break up with Trevor," she says. "I don't know."

"Yeah? How long have you been going with him?"

"Over three weeks."

"What did your mother say when she found out?"

"She didn't say anything because she doesn't know," Angelique says softly. "I didn't tell her."

"Because she'd be mad?"

"Yeah." She's quiet for a moment. "You know what? He has a gun."

"Yeah, I heard that before."

"I've seen it," she says.

We sit side by side, making one of those sand-drip castles between us, taking turns dribbling the wet sand into tall, lumpy towers. When the wind blows, the wet sand makes even funnier shapes. When I look way up the beach, I can see Robert and Trevor walking together. They look like two small specks with shimmery legs.

"So why don't you break up with him?" I ask.

"I don't know. I'm scared, I guess. He has a gang he's in. That's why he got the gun. For them. He's in the Rex. And he got a tattoo, a dinosaur head, on the inside of his arm. Besides, sometimes he's really, really nice. He gave me this." She shows me a tiny ring with a pink stone in it on her little finger.

"He doesn't mean to be so angry and nervous all the time. I guess I want to try and help him out. Like Robert does. If I tell my mom, she'll make me break up right away."

Then she gives me a little smile. "Anyway, I think it's great that you're not scared of him. He wants people to be scared of him."

We sit together for a little while, until I see Robert and Trevor getting closer. "I better go," I say, getting to my feet. "See ya."

Three

I wander back to my towel, spread it out, and lie facedown so the sun can warm my back. I want to think things over.

"Hey, where's Robert?" Tasha asks me.

"I don't know. In the water."

"Now you want to dig tunnels with me?"

"Nah. I'm not in the mood."

I thought Robert had invited me to the beach so we could be together all day. But now I see that isn't it. He's really with those other kids, not with me.

Robert and I were in school together every year since kindergarten. At the end of May, my family moved from the Auburn Street projects. And once we got settled in the new apartment, my mom didn't want me hanging around there anymore. A lot of bad stuff happens at Auburn Street—lots of stealing, lots of drugs.

My Aunt Jolita still lives in the projects with her

creepy weirdo friend Georgina. Mama had a big fight with her because she'd been stealing jewelry and didn't babysit me and Tasha the way she was supposed to. My mother won't even call her on the phone.

I know all that. But I also know that I'm not the kind of kid who's mean and bad-tempered and disrespectful. Just because my dad's in jail doesn't mean I'm automatically a criminal.

Suddenly I feel a shadow looming over me and cold water dripping on my hot back.

"Hi, Junebug. Hi, Mrs. McClain. Hi, Harriet, Tasha." Robert drops down to sit on the sand next to me.

"Hey, Robert, what's up?" I say.

"Ask your mom if you can come home with us on the bus and stay at my house for a while," he whispers. "Maybe you can sleep over."

"Oh, man. Come on, Robert. You know she won't let me." I sit up.

"Sure she will. I'll ask her myself."

Robert gets to his feet and dusts the sand off the behind of his suit. "Mrs. McClain, can Junebug ride home with me on the bus and stay over?" he says to my mom.

"No. He most certainly cannot," Mama answers.

I knew it.

"Rachel!" Harriet bursts out. "You have a lot of

friends and family who still live there, you know. Robert and Junebug haven't been able to see each other for months."

"I think Junebug should work on adjusting to our new home, that's all."

"But I did that already," I argue. "I did that soccer league."

Neither one pays any attention to me.

Harriet's good and mad. "One of these days you're going to have to start saying yes to your son and let him decide a few things for himself. You can't tell him where to go and what to do all the time. He's not his father, you know, if that's what you're worried about."

"Yes," says Mama. "That's exactly what I'm worried about."

Tasha and I glance at each other nervously. We can see how angry Mama is. She's got a pretty quick temper, but right now she holds it inside.

I can't stop myself, though. "But, Mama, I know what I'm doing. I won't turn into my dad just by sleeping over at Robert's."

"Don't interrupt me, young man. Harriet, I don't need you to tell me how to discipline my children. Especially in front of them."

"I'm sorry, Rachel. But I believe it needed saying."

We all sit there in silence. Tasha's standing in the hole she dug, holding her little shovel and watching

Mama. Tasha and I have never heard Mama and Harriet argue before.

Robert starts to walk away. He must feel awful. I know I do.

"Hey, Robert. Another time, okay?" I yell. He doesn't turn around.

The ride home is very quiet. It's late in the afternoon as we pull into Auburn Street, where Harriet has to run upstairs and pick up something for our supper. So I bet that's what the surprise is, after all, a chocolate cake. We're having a barbecue. Mama's boyfriend, Walter, is usually the chef.

I lean out the window and look across the sidewalk at the high-rise. In the middle of the plaza, two kids I used to know have a skateboard. They built a ramp with a couple of bricks and a piece of split-apart plywood. They go flying up the ramp, doing jumps in their saggy jeans, caps backward.

I look to see if the basketball hoop is still broken. Yep, still is. Poor Robert. The rim is half busted off, so it's not much good for anything. Nobody here has money to fix things up. Well, some people have money because they stole it or got it dealing drugs.

That's how you buy your life around here. Drugs. You get money and you drive a Mercedes and you get a cell phone for business. A guy I called Radar

Man covered the drug deals for Auburn Street. Everybody said he was pretty fair for a dealer, and that we could have done a whole lot worse. But he's not really fair at all. I think that's why Darnell had to run away last spring. To get away from him.

I feel funny being back in my old neighborhood. I recognize a lot of the people walking by, but they don't say hi to me, maybe because I'm in the car. I wonder if Aunt Jolita's around this afternoon. I lean out the window, looking for her.

"Hey, Mama, do you think Harriet's surprise is about Aunt Jolita?"

"No. She wouldn't fool around with something serious like that."

"Mama, are you still mad at Harriet?" Tasha asks in a small voice.

She sighs. "Oh, no. She's probably right. I guess I worry too much about you two."

"So you mean I can stay here and play with Robert?" I ask in surprise.

"Not today. But sometime."

"Really? When?" I ask.

"Junebug! Stop it."

"Sorry."

The car's hot, and it makes me feel sleepy. I lean my head back on the seat and close my eyes. I see a picture of Angelique and me sitting on the wet sand, making drip-castles.

All of a sudden, the door opens, and two big arms lift me from the car and swoop me around in a circle. I look up at a smiling face. "Darnell! You're home! You came back!" I yelp.

Mama leaps out of the car to hug him, and Tasha scrambles out of the backseat and throws herself at his legs. Darnell's mom used to babysit me when I was really little, and Darnell was like my big brother. He took me everywhere, showed me how to stay out of trouble, and taught me all his basketball moves.

"Oh, my gosh. What's up with you? Wow! What're you doing back here?" I ask in a rush.

"Doesn't school start in a few days?" He's grinning at me.

"You're going back to school? You are? Hey, Harriet, you knew Darnell was here. You knew that all day long, and you didn't tell me?"

"That's right. It was fun, too, teasing you all. Now come on. Get in, everybody. Darnell's coming over to your new house for dinner."

Darnell climbs into the back, and Tasha cuddles up on his lap. "Where did you go, Darnell?" she asks.

"I was in Boston for a few months."

"But why?"

"You know the guy you call Radar Man? Well, he lost a lot of money on a drug deal, and he wanted me and some other guys to do a robbery for him. And I said no. So that made him mad. Cause if I wasn't in on the robbery, he figured I might tell on them. It was like he didn't have enough control over me. So I went away for a while. Up in Boston, I got a job at the Aquarium, scrubbing the sea turtle's back with a brush, cleaning up after penguins. It was smelly, but fun."

"What grade are you going into, Darnell?" Mama asks as she slowly and carefully drives past the library, the city green, the courthouse. "Eleventh?"

"Yeah. I'm sixteen, remember? Listen, Junebug, I learned one thing while I was working at the Aquarium. You gotta go to college if you want any kind of a life at all besides Mickey Dee's. I'm gonna study computers or maybe law."

"Law? Wait a minute. What about the NBA?"

He stops talking, stares at me. "Wait a minute, yourself! No. Okay, I get this. I know what's going on. Are you still hanging out with that kid, Robert? Is that why you said that?"

"Yeah. I guess."

"Well, first of all, Robert's friends with Trevor now, Junebug. You know that?"

"Yeah," I mumble.

"And second, that NBA stuff is total bull. It's nothing but TV and daydreams. You gotta live a life that you can make real, or you'll be shoveling penguin poop forever."

I sit back, much more quiet. Darnell's changed, I guess. He didn't use to say stuff like that. He didn't use to have such a strong opinion. But I respect Darnell more than anybody. He always tells me the truth.

Four

We're a little late getting back to the house, and Walter's blue pickup truck with the words ASHFORD CONSTRUCTION COMPANY on the side is already parked at the curb. The truck says Ashford because Walter is Reverend Ashford's son.

I can see a little curly string of smoke rising up behind the apartments from our backyard grill. I bet anything Walter's barbecuing spare ribs already. When it comes to barbecuing, Walter is the king. He makes good pizza, too.

The spare ribs and fresh corn turn out great. After the dinner clean-up, Darnell and I go outside and stretch out on the grass.

"Junebug, your mom's new boyfriend, he's cool. He's an awesome cook. He's going to teach me how to make some real hot salsa."

"Yeah."

But my voice is flat. I wish I wanted to learn how

to make salsa. But I don't. Walter's running our bar-becue grill as if he lives here with us. As if he's a member of the family. Well, he's not. I already have a dad.

"Darnell, have you ever seen your father?" I ask.

"Yeah. Lots of times. When I was little mostly. We used to go to church a lot, I know that. But that was a long time ago. After church, he used to take me to my grandmother's house, and we'd have a great big meal with gravy and corn bread and stuff like that. Now he's moved. To North Carolina. He has new kids and a new wife. I could go visit if I wanted, but it's kind of awkward with his new kids."

I sit up, frowning. "If your dad was in jail, would you visit him?"

"I guess so. Maybe I would . . . like at Christmas."

"Christmas? Why?"

"I don't know. It would be like giving him a pres-ent."

"That's the only time you'd go?"

"Yeah. Probably. What's up with you, anyway?"

"Nothing. I don't want Walter thinking he can just take over around here. I guess I want to call my real dad and talk to him," I mumble.

"Yeah? Well, why don't you, then?"

"Oh, because Mama doesn't want us to have any-thing to do with him. And I don't want to make Mama mad. If I call him, then she might think—"

"You mean she'll think you don't appreciate her and you're going behind her back?" Darnell says.

"Yeah."

Boy, I'd missed having Darnell around to talk to. That's exactly the problem. If I want to talk to my dad, I know I'll be choosing between two parents, between being loyal to my mom and finding out about my father.

"Actually, I'm pretty sure you have to write a letter first and tell the prisoner to make the call out," Darnell says slowly. "Prisons don't take phone messages for inmates."

So I'll have to write him. Maybe that's a good idea. I can send a letter, and then if he doesn't call, I'll know he's forgotten us for good. And if he does call here, I won't have the trouble of trying to get ahold of him in some great big prison.

"Are you sure about that?" I ask.

"Yeah. Trust me. By my age, you'll have friends in jail. That's how you reach them. They can only call out at certain times, too. They can't call during lockdowns, which is like after mealtimes and exercise periods."

Last year all the kids in my class knew who their dads were. Whenever I see Walter with Mama, I start wondering what my real dad looks like. I can't really remember. Mama didn't keep any photographs of him or anything. What does his voice sound like? Am

I going to be like him when I grow up? I have to know. I have to.

Just from talking about it, a heavy feeling floats off my shoulders, and I get the urge to start a big wrestle. So I get on my knees and launch myself at Darnell.

"Oof. Hey! Not now. Lay off, you ten-ton elephant. I'm digesting." Darnell groans.

The grownups, Mama, Harriet, and Walter, come out with a pitcher of lemonade and sit on the steps, talking softly as the sun goes down. They look as if they're doing fine. And my mom looks so happy. I know she doesn't want me to call my dad. But I know now that somehow I'm going to.

"Hey, Darnell. Think you could mail a note to my dad for me and ask him to call? I don't have the address for the prison."

He thinks for a minute. "Yeah. Okay. But you know, it might not be as easy as you think. It could take a while for him to get the letter."

"That's okay."

If Darnell helps me, all I have to do is write my dad. He'll call me right back. Easy as pie. I'm going to do it right now.

"I'll be back in a minute, Darnell." I leap to my feet and run for the door. "Excuse me, Mama." She's sitting on the stoop, blocking the door. "Gotta use the bathroom."

I run into my bedroom and pull a piece of paper

out of my school supply pack. My dad's at the East Bridgton Correctional Facility, I do know that much. Mama says it's not a jail. It's a prison. Once I looked in the dictionary to find out the difference. A jail is where you go just for a little while, before your hearing, when the judge decides if you've got a case that needs a trial. A prison is where you go to stay when you're found guilty. My dad's staying ten years, but he's finished more than half of it.

> Dear Dad,
>
> I bet you are surprised to hear from me. Well, I wanted to see how you are doing. Tasha and I start school on Wednesday. I'm in fifth grade now. I know you have our phone number. Maybe you can call us real soon.
>
> Love,
> Reeve McClain, Jr.

I fold up the paper and hurry back outside. Darnell puts the letter in his pocket.

Now Miss Williams comes outside for some lemonade. And soon Mrs. Upset-Tummy Johnson and Uncle Tim with the bristly red eyebrows join the grownups. Of all the elderly Mama takes care of, Tasha and I like Miss Williams the best. She taught me some tai chi. Miss Williams is cool. Even though she's tiny, she's tough. I happen to know that Reverend Ashford likes her, too.

In a low voice, Darnell says, "Hey, Junebug, you know Richie Payne?"

"Huh? Oh, yeah, sure I do."

Richie's seventeen years old, living at Auburn Street on the eighth floor, one floor below our old apartment. His parents used to fight something awful. You could hear them at night.

"He did a drive-by shooting. Killed somebody, too. He had a semiautomatic, an AK-47. The police were all over the place last week. No one knows where Richie went. No one's talking. He might even be dead. His mother's crying her heart out. But I guess it's kind of late for that."

"Did the police question you?"

"Yeah. Your Aunt Jolita, too. Everybody."

Neither of us says anything for a while. Now we're locked in a place that's only for poor kids. Teenagers. A lot of guys follow the Richie path—not going home ever, not going to school. Who can blame them? I wouldn't go home either, if I was Richie.

The grownups keep talking and laughing, relaxing. They don't notice me and Darnell sitting so quietly in the grass. When I think about what Richie Payne's done, my heart feels squeezed in my chest—that old sick-to-my-stomach feeling I used to have back at Auburn Street. That's what guns do to you. When you know half the guys around you are carrying, you feel hopeless and scared. It means guys don't know of any other way to fix things but by pulling the trigger. Just like in the movies. Blow 'em away. Blow 'em up. Bodies falling everywhere. Mel Gibson. Eddie Murphy. Danny Glover. Bruce Willis.

I want to cry about Richie. I want to scream about Richie. I look at Darnell.

He says, "It's bad, huh."

I nod. When I think of all that stuff I left behind at Auburn Street, my head wants to explode. If Robert keeps hanging around Trevor, what will happen to him? Will he even survive?

"Darnell, did any of your friends ever get killed?"

"Yeah. Some. I've been to six funerals."

Later, while I'm lying in bed, I wonder if I should tell Mama about Trevor being in the Rex and having a gun. But around here everyone's always super busy, and I don't want her to worry about me so much.

The next morning, my eyes fly open early, and I can't get back to sleep. Now that I gave Darnell that letter to mail, I'm going to have to tell Mama what I did. What if the phone rings one afternoon, and it's Dad? I can't have her find out about the letter that way. I have to tell her that I went behind her back, and who can go back to sleep when he's thinking about something like that? Not me.

Five

On Wednesday, school starts, fifth grade, and it's no big deal. This kid I don't like, Greg, completely ignores me, even though we both have Mr. Olson, our teacher from the year before. I like Mr. Olson a lot. But he starts out pretty strict. On the first day of school, we have homework! And it's not just covering our books with paper-bag covers. He gives us forty math problems besides. And we have to write a poem.

I want to write about guns. I make a list of rhymes. Fun. Bun. Run. Sun. Ton. I'm trying to write a rap. But first I want to think of a rhyme for *bullet*. And I can't.

Time to take a break! I go to the phone and call Robert.

"Hey! How'd you do at school today?" I ask.

"Okay. Except they gave us a list of stuff to buy. How am I going to do that? Remember, your mom always bought stuff for both of us together?"

"Yeah. Hey, you want to sleep over here Friday night?" We hardly had any time together. I want to make up for our bad day at the beach. Maybe Mama can help him get his school supplies.

"Sure. I can bring a couple of monster videos."

"Not those *King Kong* ones again."

"Why not? I like them."

"We've seen them a million times."

"Yeah, but they're great!"

After I hang up, I go back to writing my rap poem. It's pretty easy.

Time 2 Stop

U think it's great
U think it's cool?
We're the only country
U get shot at school.
Out on the playground
Bullets are flying
And that's the way
the children are dying.
Who needs a cop
to tell 'em to stop?
U know what's wrong
U know what's right
Now is the time
To end this fight.

I try to read my rap poem to Mama, but she's busy doing paperwork for Medicare or Medicaid or something. So I zip across the hall and read it to Miss Williams and Tasha. Miss Williams likes it a lot, and Tasha hops up and does a little dance to the beat. We'll have to see what Mr. Olson says. I bet he's going to tell me it's much too short.

I put away my schoolwork and wander outside with my basketball. As usual, there's nothing to do around here. No hoop. No kids. It's so boring. I sit on the bench for a minute. I wonder if Darnell mailed the letter for me. I wander back inside. Mama's watching *Oprah*. That's good. *Oprah* lasts an hour.

"I'm going to call Darnell," I say.

She barely looks at me. "Okay."

I flop down on her bed and dial his number.

"Hey, Darnell. It's me!"

"Junebug! You wild and crazy guy. What's up?"

"I wondered if you mailed that letter for me."

"Of course I did. Your dad didn't call yet?"

"No. Do you think he will?" I ask.

"I have no idea, Junebug."

"What are you doing?"

"Right now?" Darnell laughs. "Homework. Reading Shakespeare, actually. It beats the pants off cleaning up after penguins."

"Did anything happen yet with Richie Payne?" I ask.

"Yeah. The police kept hanging around, questioning everybody. Door-to-door, just about. Nobody knew where he was. But the detectives kept coming around, looking for a lead, anything. They stopped me on the street and questioned me. Stopped my brother Gabe, too. And then finally, Richie turned himself in at the police station."

"He did?" I sure didn't expect that. "How come?"

"He felt bad about what he'd done. He committed murder, Junebug. He planned and carried out a drive-by shooting. That's murder."

"Yeah," I say, a cold feeling blowing inside me. "But why did he do it, Darnell? Just cause some other kids told him to?"

"Who knows why? He should know not to do what someone else says. He's old enough to know better. Probably he was on drugs or drunk."

"Do you think that Trevor, when he gets older . . . Do you think he might do something that bad?" I ask.

"Why are you even talking about that kid? Didn't I tell you to stay away from him?"

"I saw him at the beach. I didn't hang out with him, though."

"Yeah? Well, make that the last time you see him. Listen, I gotta go now."

"Okay. Bye."

On Friday, Robert comes over. Since Mama can't go pick him up, he takes the bus across town and shows up at my door around five. He's carrying an entire gym bag full of tapes, videos, candy, baseball and football cards—you name it. And he's just in time for dinner.

"Hi, Mrs. McClain. Hi, Tasha. How's first grade treating you?"

"I get homework now the same as Junebug," Tasha says.

"You do? No way."

"Yeah, I do. See?"

She hands over a page she's supposed to be doing with her crayons, matching colors and numbers to fill in a clown holding balloons.

"Nice. Hey, you're growing taller, right?" Robert asks her.

She grins. "Yeah. And I can beat Junebug up, too. I take tai chi."

"Just ignore her," I tell Robert. "She's really been getting out of line."

"No, no. This is cool. Can you beat me up, Tasha?"

"Yeah. Easy."

"Okay, then. Do it. Come on, Tash. Show me your stuff."

Tasha backs up a couple of steps, goes into the cat stance, weight on her back foot, heel up on her front foot, takes a couple of really deep breaths, raises her hands into position, and—

"No way, young lady!" Mama says, grabbing her wrist. I fall onto the sofa, laughing.

"Not now, Tasha. You can roughhouse outside later on. We're going to eat." Mama marches her to the table.

Robert and I have to do the dinner dishes. Tasha is scraper and carrier. She also has to take out the soggy old trash. Ha, ha, ha.

"Did I tell you I'm thinking about joining the Rex?" Robert says quietly. "Next year, maybe."

I screw my face up. "Oh, come on, man! Cut it out. I thought we had this settled about Trevor and that dumb gang. You gotta stay in school. Get good grades. You can't go out running around like he does. You have to get to all the practices for b-ball."

"Yeah, well let me ask you this. How? How am I going to get to practices and do my homework? We had our electricity cut off three times this summer. And the phone, too. And when they come to try to collect the rent, the man asks where my mama's at. What am I supposed to tell him? That I don't know? That I haven't seen her in three days? I can't tell anyone that. They'll put me in foster care for sure. What's it to you what I do, Junebug? You don't even live at Auburn Street anymore."

"Cut it out with this what-does-it-matter crap!" I am really angry. "What does it matter where I live? We're brothers, right? How can you forget that? Remember the vow we signed when school got out?"

41

"The one we signed with the red food coloring?" He smiles.

"Yeah. I swore I'd always help you out. So I'm helping you now. I'm giving you good advice. You better listen to me. You gotta be ready for the NBA scouts, Robert. I'm counting on you. If you keep practicing the way you do now, they'll take you for sure."

"Maybe. But what if they pass me by? Did you ever think about that? How many kids do they send up?"

"Yeah," I say slowly, remembering what Darnell told me.

"I need something I can count on. Trevor'll watch out for me. He already said so."

"But Trevor's not gonna . . . the Rex doesn't care . . ."

Robert glares at me. "Just shut up. Forget it. Cause the truth is, nobody really cares, nobody besides you. And you can't help me. You're just a kid."

This is as close as Robert and I ever came to a really bad argument. But he can't go with the Rex. He can't. I can be as stubborn as Tasha or Mama any day. Or worse. Then Mama comes in to wipe down the counters. So we stop talking.

I watch the dishwater go down the drain in a swirl of bubbles. All I know is, if you go with a gang, you start doing whatever it is they tell you to do. First it's little things like errands—that's for fifth-graders, maybe sixth. If there's a fight, you have to prove you're willing to do anything. After sixth grade, you have to do some stealing or deliver dope for a drug guy. You don't even think about it. The man just says, "Come here, kid." And you go on over and say, "Yeah?" And he gives you ten dollars. That's how it starts. That's how it started with Trevor. I know because I was there when it happened.

Six

Later, around ten o'clock, Robert and I pull our blankets and pillows into the living room. Robert brought a bag of marshmallows and a flashlight and a whole bunch of other stuff.

"What's with all the marshmallows?" I ask.

He pulls out two carefully arranged packs of football cards and two dice. "Wait till you see this. First, who do you want to be, the Cowboys or the Patriots?"

"The Cowboys, I guess. Hey! Yuck! What are you doing?"

Robert takes a marshmallow and squishes it with his fingers. He shapes it into a little football and sets it on the carpet. I have to laugh.

"That ball's on the fifty-yard line," he announces.

I take the rubber band off my card pack. I'm holding two entire Cowboy lineups, offensive and defensive. Robert has the Patriot lineup.

"All right," Robert says, "we're playing marshmallow football. When your quarterback card throws the pass, he has to hit the receiver card in the chest for the pass to be completed, okay?"

"Okay." I start to laugh.

"Now you have to think up six offensive plays and write them down. Those are your choices. And when you roll the dice, say it's a four, then that's your play. Got it?"

"Look at this sorry thing!"

I pick up the mashed-up football. I pull my arm back like a quarterback about to throw a pass. "The tight end goes deep. He's looking . . ." I start laughing again and roll over on the floor.

"Come on, man, play this right," Robert says, but he's smiling, too. "Write down your six plays, but don't show me."

"Yeah? Okay, but where are the refs?"

"I'm the refs."

"You can't be all of them!" I argue.

"I'll be fair, Junebug. Don't worry about that."

"You think I'm worried about marshmallow football?"

"Yeah. You're suffering from stress. You have pregame jitters," Robert says.

Robert has a great imagination. We always have fun when he sleeps over.

We finally get in a few rounds of marshmallow football. Then I ask him what movie he brought.

"We will be skipping *King Kong* due to viewer complaints. But this is an excellent one," Robert says. "It's called *The Spider That Ate Manhattan.*"

We put it in the VCR. First there's some terrible music. Then we see the police station, in grainy black and white, everyone running around out of their minds with fear. And then—the spider! The spider is so fake-looking it's hilarious. It has long, bristly hairs all over it like a bathroom cleaning brush. We can't stop laughing.

Mama comes out of her room. "Boys, come on. It's after eleven o'clock."

"Okay. Okay. It's almost over."

We try to quiet down, but when the spider starts climbing up the Empire State Building and sticking his fake-looking bristly legs in the windows of people's offices, we laugh so hard that Mama has to come out of her room again and stop the movie.

"You can watch the rest tomorrow," she says firmly.

It's probably a good thing she turns it off. Laughing has become a disease. I've been laughing so much that my ribs hurt, and I forget all about Robert joining the Rex until I lie down, and the room is dark and quiet.

"Hey, Robert?" I whisper. I shine my flashlight on him. He's almost asleep. Ooops.

"Get that light off me, Junebug."

I switch off the flashlight. "You won't really join Trevor's gang, will you?" I whisper.

"I don't know. Yeah. Probably."

I don't know what to say. "Why?" I ask again. How can he think like this?

"Why? Who do I have on my side? I already explained this to you. So just get over it."

"But you can come here anytime you want, Robert. I swear. Anytime in your whole entire life."

"That's what you say now. I bet you won't be saying it in a month or two. How come you never came over to play when I asked you before?"

I feel bad. "My mother wouldn't let me cause there was no supervision," I mumble. "She says it's time for me to get used to being here."

"Yeah, I know what she thinks. Well, I really needed you to come over. My mom, you know how she stays out late a lot and has a lot of boyfriends? It's been really bad this summer, Junebug. Really bad."

I lean up on one elbow. "What kind of bad?"

"Like drinking and hitting and stuff."

"Really? Maybe you should tell someone. Like Harriet. Or my mom. Or Darnell."

"And what would your mother say? She'd be asking me questions. You know that. She'd probably call Social Services. Promise you won't tell her, all right? Now I gotta get some sleep."

He turns over, a big, long lump in the sleeping bag. I lie awake on my back, thinking about Richie Payne and Trevor. I feel heartsick about Robert choosing those guys over me. Because once he finally goes with them and the Rex, it's gotta be all for one.

I lie awake for a long time, trying to think of a way to help Robert.

Seven

Saturday night, we're eating one of Walter's pizzas, and I pull off a big wad of melted mozzarella cheese. I'm shaping it into a gooey little football. Then I cock my arm, elbow up, like a quarterback. "He's back. He's deep. He's looking . . ." I can tell Walter is trying not to smile.

"Junior. Stop playing with your food. Are you in nursery school?" Mama says.

"No. Hey, Mama, I have to tell you something. It's . . . well, actually . . . I want to talk to my dad."

I keep my eyes down, afraid to look up and see if she's angry. But I know she is. "So I—I sent a letter. I mean, Darnell sent a letter to the prison asking Dad to call here."

There's silence at the table. My heart is pounding.

"You went behind my back?" Mama's voice is hard and cold. "If your father had wanted to call us, June-

49

bug, he could have. Anytime. But since he didn't, ever, I don't want you talking to him, especially without checking with me first."

"Now, Rachel, hold on," Walter says. "Can we discuss this for a minute? I mean, maybe it's not such a bad idea. I'm sure Reeve has a lot of questions about his dad. Especially since he's the kind of kid who does nothing but ask questions."

I look at him gratefully, and he gives me an encouraging smile. Darnell's right, as usual. Walter's pretty cool.

"You're kidding me," Mama says to Walter, tilting her head to one side. "You really think it's a good idea? How so?"

"Because it's normal. It's natural for kids, and not just kids, to wonder about things like that. Who their parents are, what they're like."

Mama puts down her fork.

"I just don't want to see my kids get hurt any more than they already have been. I know what this man is like, Walter. You don't."

"But, Mama, I was thinking maybe we could talk on the phone once in a while. And I could send him some photos of me and Tasha, so he can remember us," I add. "Anyway, Darnell sent the letter last week."

"Well," she says, shaking her head doubtfully, "okay. But he may never call, so don't get your hopes up, Junior. Please."

"I won't."

But it's too late! My hopes are already as high as a kite!

The next night at dinner, we have plain old pork chops and beans because Walter didn't come over. I get busy with the ketchup, squirting it on everything until Mama takes it out of my hands.

Mama says, "I wish your father would go ahead and call. I'd like to get this over with."

Then, right at the end of the six-thirty news, the phone rings, and I just know deep down that it's him. Mama and I look at each other.

She said she'd help me with the call, so I guess this is it. "Ready?" she asks.

I nod. My mouth is dry, so dry I have to clear my throat. My tongue feels big and stuck. A million thoughts fly through my mind at once.

That word *lockdown* that Darnell used. That was scary.

Mama smiles at me when she sees how scared I am. She gives me a quick hug and takes the receiver. I sit close to her so I can hear.

The operator asks Mama if she will accept a collect call from Reeve McClain. I close my eyes when I hear that. I feel a swirl of dizziness go through me. That's my name, but it's not me. It's somebody I hardly know, I hardly remember. Reeve McClain is a wide, dark empty hole, an outer-space place. I move away from the phone.

"Hello?" Mama says in a nervous voice. "Is this Reeve? Reeve McClain? This is Rachel. Hi. You doing okay? Good, good. Right. Yeah. Long time no see. Yeah, I'm fine. Here. Hold on a second. I've got someone who wants to talk to you."

She hands me the receiver.

"Hello? Dad?"

"Well, Reeve Junior! Is that you?"

"Yeah."

"You sound good. Damn."

I don't know what to say. This is much harder than I thought. "I mean, are— How's— Are you okay?" I ask.

"Well, yeah. Sure. I'm doing real good. Considering. How's Tasha?"

"Fine. She started first grade."

"My baby in first grade? And what grade are you in?"

He doesn't know? He doesn't know what grade I'm in? I just sent him a letter telling him! "Fifth."

"Wow. You kids are growing up fast. You're growing up without me, aren't you? Well, that's what everybody on the inside says, their kids grow up without them. I bet you're tall now, huh?"

"Not really. Not too tall. Some girls in my class are taller than I am."

"Oh, yeah?" He laughs. "I remember that stage. You into sports? You like boxing?"

"Boxing? No. Not really."

"Boxing's a great workout. You ought to give it a try. The heavy bag, man, you best make no mistakes with that thing. It'll come right back at ya every time."

"I had a job this summer—"

"Oh, yeah? Good for you. That's real good. Hey, put your mother back on. No. Wait. Listen, Junior, I want to tell you something. I'm not guilty. No matter what they say, I was just in the wrong place at the wrong time. All right?"

"Yeah. Well, bye, Dad."

"Bye now. I'll call you next week, all right? You be good."

Be good? Is that all he has to tell me? He doesn't even want to hear about my job? He can't remember what grade I'm in?

Instead of getting on herself, Mama ushers Tasha into the bedroom and hands her the phone. Tasha's scowling and holding on to Theo for dear life. She's acting like her old shy, stubborn self.

"Hi," she whispers into the phone. "Are you Dad?"

"What on earth? Of course he's Dad," I sputter.

Mama hushes me.

"I'm in first grade," she says. "And I know tai chi karate," she adds.

I roll my eyes at Mama, and she smiles.

"You want to talk to Theo now? He's my teddy bear." Tasha puts Theo on the phone. For Pete's sake.

Mama quickly takes the receiver. She asks him a

couple of questions just to be polite, like does he read or exercise. And then that's it. She hangs up and smiles at us brightly. "Well. Is that what you expected? It went okay, right?" Mama asks.

I nod. "Yeah. It was good." But I don't feel that way. I feel angry. Or maybe sad. I can't tell. I feel hot and crazy inside.

I hurry into my bedroom, grabbing Theo on the way. Tasha lets me use him in emergencies. I shut the door and take a running dive for my bed.

I'm angry at my dad. Really angry.

"Be good." Why should I be good? He's not good. Probably he *is* guilty of robbery. Probably Mama is right. He says he didn't do it. But I don't believe him.

How come he doesn't have time to talk to me, even now? After two sentences, he wanted to talk to Mama, not me. And I'm the one who wrote him.

And then I wonder again, did he really do it? Did he rob a store? With a gun? Instead of fewer questions about him, I have more. And I have a whopping headache. Maybe it was better not knowing anything.

Eight

On the first Sunday in October, Darnell and Harriet come over around noon. Later we're going to take a ride to the country to buy pumpkins for Halloween and some cider. Harriet brought her camera so she can leap out of the car and take pictures of the red and yellow autumn trees.

After we eat, I start talking with Darnell as he flips TV channels, looking for the play-off game. Darnell's a Yankee fan. He thinks their rookie shortstop, Derek Jeter, is cool. I guess I'm for the Texas team, the Rangers. But actually, I couldn't care less about baseball.

"So, guess what. I never called to tell you this, but I did it, Darnell. I talked to my dad."

He flicks off the sound, some wavery-voiced lady singing the national anthem, and looks at me. "Whoa! That's major. That's huge. How did it go?"

"I don't know. Not great. I didn't really know what to say."

"Yeah? That's not surprising. I bet he didn't know what to say, either."

"You think so?"

"It would take a lot of time to get used to each other after six years. Think about it."

"Yeah. Maybe it was a dumb idea in the first place, writing to him."

"No. Probably he feels awkward on the phone. Maybe you should stick to writing— Whoa! Hold it, Junebug. Jeter's up. The Yankees are going to crush the Rangers." Darnell leans forward and turns the volume up again. "Come on, Jeter."

I feel a little gloomy, a little sorry for myself. I can't tell Darnell it's been four weeks since my dad called. He said he'd call again, but he didn't.

We sit for a while, watching the first inning. Neither of us speaks. But it's a comfortable quiet. As the game progresses, Darnell relaxes some more and stretches out on the sofa. I try to pay attention, but the game is so boring! I want to do something else.

"Hey, Darnell. Want to go up to the field and play soccer for a while?" I ask.

"Soccer? Sure. You can show me your moves. Where's the field?"

"Just up the hill behind the bakery. Not far."

We run up to the field where I had soccer league in the summer. It's completely deserted. We have the whole place to ourselves. There's only a man walking a little white, woolly dog over at the far end.

Darnell and I take turns being goalie while one of us takes shots on goal. Then Darnell wants me to show him how I bounce the ball off my head. I watch the ball coming and lean into it, using the top of my forehead, jumping up a little on my toes. The ball pops high into the air. Most players use heading to clear the goal area. At least as a fullback, that was what I was supposed to do.

Just then, I notice a police car pulling up to the curb next to the field. The cruiser stops. Two policemen get out. One white, one black. They start slowly walking—straight toward us!

I tuck the ball under my arm and jog over to Darnell. "Look. Police. Why are they coming here, Darnell?"

"I don't know. But I bet you anything it's not to play soccer with us. Here, Junebug, give me the ball. Quick, now, take my wallet, okay? Slip it into your back pocket so they can't see you doing it."

I want to ask why in the worst way, but I don't. We start walking over to the policemen and meet them near the sidelines.

"Hi," Darnell says. "Is there something we can help you with?"

"Yeah. Why don't you two walk to the car with us," the black one says.

"Why?" Darnell asks. "Is something wrong?"

"There was a break-in in the area. One of the businesses reported a robbery about a half hour ago."

"A robbery? We've been out here playing soccer!" I burst out.

I don't get this at all.

"Okay. Then you won't mind us searching your buddy, will you?"

I can feel Darnell's anger more than I can see it.

"Step up to the car, son, and lean forward," the black policeman says.

"What is this?" Darnell bursts out bitterly, speaking to the black policeman. "They got a brother like you doing their dirty work, too?"

"Hey! Watch your mouth, kid. Arms up, fella. Spread your legs. Come on." The white one prods Darnell in the back so hard that he falls forward onto the car.

The police start patting him down, all up and down his legs, around front, their hands pressing against him. Two cars go by, driving real slow so they can get a good look at us. I am so embarrassed that I want to cry. Why do they think I would rob somebody, some store? I would *never* do that. Are they out of their minds?

"Do you have any ID?" they ask Darnell.

"Not on me."

58

"Let me see your wallet," the white one says.

"Didn't bring it with me to play soccer."

They look at each other. The black one shrugs. "All right, boys. That's it for now."

They get back into the patrol car and drive slowly off. They turn left at the far end of the field, where the man is still walking the dog. They drive right by him without stopping.

"Hey! They didn't stop and talk to him!" I yell. "That's not fair."

"Yeah. That's because he's white," Darnell says. "Is that the first time you've seen the police search someone, Junebug?"

"Yeah. But why did they?"

"Cause when they see young black guys, if there's any crime in the area, you get stopped for it while they check you out. Even if there isn't a crime—say you're driving slow for some reason—they'll stop you. You gotta get used to it and not lose your cool. Don't tell your mother about this, though, or she'll worry to death. It's nothing serious, okay? The best thing to do is forget about it. Now listen, we have to get back so you can go get your Halloween stuff."

"You want your wallet back?"

"Oh, yeah. Thanks."

"Why did you want me to hold it?"

"Cause I've still got a fake driver's license in there. The one that says I'm eighteen, so I could get the Aquarium job in Boston. But you know what? That was wrong of me to ask you to hold it. I should just get rid of that ID."

We start walking down the hill. Now I'm curious. "Is that how they questioned you about Richie Payne? The police were driving around and stopped you on the street?"

"Yeah."

I have one more question. "Darnell, did you ever get arrested for real?"

"Yeah. Once."

"How old were you?"

"Seventh grade."

"Really? Wow. What did you do?"

"A bunch of us tried smoking weed after school, and the vice principal caught us. Most of the kids managed to run away, but I stayed, trying to do the honest thing, you know? I'm kind of a lightning rod for trouble. You better keep away from me, June-bug!"

I burst out laughing.

"Forget about those cops, okay? We were just in the wrong place at the wrong time." He swats my head. "Come on. Race ya."

Darnell takes the bus home, and Harriet drives us north on little winding roads to a farmstand where they sell pumpkins. During the ride, I start thinking about what happened with the police. How mad I felt when they were patting Darnell down. How he said the very same thing my dad had said—about being in the wrong place at the wrong time. That could get you in trouble? Just that? Maybe. They never even stopped the white guy, and he was in the same place, the same time as we were.

We find the farmstand. They sell hundreds of pumpkins heaped on a flat trailer. A lot of families are there, the kids racing around, everyone looking for the right pumpkin to carve.

The pumpkins are every kind of shape—round, tall, peanut-shaped, lopsided. I don't care. I still feel ashamed, remembering those cars driving by really slow up at the playing field, watching while the police have Darnell pushed up against the car, his face turned sideways. They're all watching, thinking we're juvenile delinquents, criminals.

How could the police ever think I would break into a building? No, I know why. It's because kids like Trevor *do* break into buildings. And then the police think I'm just any old black kid and not me, Junebug.

"Junior! What is with you?" Mama asks sharply. "I've asked you three times already—is that really the pumpkin you want?"

"Huh? Yeah. This one."

I'm holding a lopsided, greenish one with a rotten spot on the bottom. It's the ugliest pumpkin in the world. But right now, I like it. It's perfect.

Nine

At school, the weeks have gone by fast. I really like being in Mr. O.'s class again, and with Greg ignoring me, fifth grade is a breeze. I'm even sitting around with extra time on my hands. Mr. Olson says he might recommend me for a gifted program. I'll go—as long as we don't have to watch baseball, eat asparagus, or sing.

Around six-thirty on October 14, a Monday, my dad finally calls again. This time Tasha talks to him for about one minute.

"Hi, Dad. You know what? Mama takes care of old people here. And Miss Williams is my friend. I'm going to be a fireman—no, I mean a firewoman—for Halloween. You want to talk to Junebug now?"

She hands me the phone. "Hi, Dad."

"How's school?" he asks.

"Fine. It's easy."

"Yeah? Doing the work is easy, or skipping the work is easy?" He laughs at his own joke.

"I do the work!" I don't want him teasing me about being a good student.

"Listen, let me have your mother again. I want to ask her if you all can come up here and visit this Saturday."

"A visit? Me and Tasha?" Oh, man. I don't know how Mama will take this.

"Sure. Put her on, okay?"

I hand Mama the phone and head for the rocking chair. Go see Dad this Saturday? What's she going to say?

To my surprise, she says yes.

East Bridgton Correctional Facility is two hours' drive from our house. Walter picks me and Mama up at seven o'clock in the morning. We're not bringing Tasha. She's staying with her friend Ruthie. She felt kind of left out at first, but she got over it. I think she would be scared once we got there.

We head northwest. North of Danbury someplace. When we get there, I'm surprised by the number of cars in the parking lot. Probably a hundred prisoners inside have Saturday visitors.

There are towers at each corner of a high stone prison wall, and rolls of barbed wire curl along the tops of the walls between the towers. In each tower stand two guards, one with a rifle. I sink into the backseat so I can't see them, so they can't see me. This looks like a place for a war.

Walter walks us all the way to the visitors' entrance. Then he gives Mama a kiss and me a hug and says he'll meet us in an hour. I wish he were coming with us. I'm worried about everything. How will we find my dad? How will we recognize him? How will I know what to say? What if he and Mama get into an argument? What if Mama and I get into an argument? I don't want to go in.

"Now, listen, don't hurry," Walter says to us. "Take all the time you need. I won't be going anywhere."

And when he says that, for some reason, I feel better. I guess I feel like Walter's my way out.

He gives me a quick pat on the shoulder and heads for the car. I try to take a big, relaxing breath, but my chest feels tight as a drum. We head for the prison door. I'm holding Mama's hand. I don't care how old I am. I do not want to get separated from her in here. What if I got locked in by mistake?

There's a short line ahead of us waiting to go in. We stand at the end.

"Hey, Mama, Dad says he's innocent. He told me that a couple of times."

"I know. He told me, too."

"Well, if he's innocent, then why is he in here?"

"I guess for an innocent man, he was doing something wrong."

"What if the judge made a mistake? Can that happen? Or is the judge always right?"

"I don't know if judges are always right. I think they're supposed to be fair, though. Hush for now. We have to sign in at this window. Put down the time and your signature." She signs the list.

"Me, too?"

"Sure."

I look around. I can't help but notice that there are mostly very, very poor people here. We look like the richest ones. I never thought I was rich before.

We stand on another line so we can be checked by security. Then we go through an electronic X-ray gate, then past more guards on either side, and finally through two huge metal doors with wire covering the windows. Everything is painted a dull whitish green, a really ugly color. There are no paintings or calendars, no posters. Nothing to look at.

There are a few chairs inside the waiting room, but they're already taken, one by a huge fat lady. Her feet puff out over the edges of her penny loafers. Her husband stands next to her, a little teeny-tiny guy in a gray suit. They look like Jack Sprat and his wife. If I look at them one more second, I'm going to explode laughing, and I don't think I'll be able to stop. I can get very giggly when I'm this nervous. I turn the other way, quick, and start to think about the prison.

Jail sounds short and a little bit cheerful. Not so bad. It rhymes with *pail*. But *prison*, that sounds bad.

To pass the time, I try to think of rhymes for it, but I can't.

We stand there, waiting. It's noisy and echoey and no one looks happy. It's like being in a nasty hospital. Another metal door opens.

"Reeve and Rachel McClain," a woman guard shouts. She's wearing police-style pants and has a gun in a holster.

"That's us," Mama says.

"I think I know that," I say.

"Wise guy." She gives my hand a squeeze. "Let's go."

Ten

The guard escorts us quickly, too quickly, into a tiny room with a countertop, two chairs, and a big glass window. The room on the other side of the glass is empty. Dad's not here!

"Hey, where's my dad?" I ask the guard.

"Just take a seat. He'll be here. Don't worry."

"How do I open this window?" I ask.

Mama picks up the black-handled phone attached to the table by a cable. She shows it to me. My mouth goes dry, just the way it did the first time Dad called.

"You talk to him through this," Mama says. "He'll be using a phone on the other side."

"Oh. Okay."

My heart is racing. I crack my knuckles to stay calm.

"Is Dad kept on the other side of the glass because the guards are afraid he'll hurt us?" I ask.

I'm even more scared. I never thought about him being violent before. Did he ever hurt Mama? Is that why she doesn't want to stay married to him?

"I think it's mostly so we can't give him things he's not supposed to have," Mama says.

"Like escaping tools?"

"Right."

We sit there, waiting for what seems like years, but Mama says it's fifteen minutes. I put the phone down and wipe my sweaty palms on my pants. Through the window, we see the door open, and a guard waves the prisoner to a seat before he quickly shuts the door. And there we are, locked in, face to face with my dad.

Quickly he comes over to the chair and takes the phone. "Hey! Hi, Rachel, hi, Reeve. What's happening, buddy?"

He's big. My dad is big! Tall. Tall enough for basketball! He's wearing a bright orange prison shirt over a clean white T-shirt and baggy pants, and he looks like he has a lot of muscles. I heard that guys work out and lift a lot in prison.

"Nothing much."

"Where's Tasha?" he asks.

"She stayed home because it's so far. It took us—"

But he interrupts. Already he's talking again: "Rachel, how are you?"

I hand Mama the phone, but his voice is so loud that I can hear, too.

"It's great to see you. You look incredible. Listen, maybe in a few months, I'll be out of this place and transferred to a minimum-security facility. Then it'll be a lot easier to visit. A real room, no glass window."

"Oh, well, that's nice." Mama smiles a little, but it's sure not the kind of smile she gives Walter. And right then I know that Dad is still thinking about her. Maybe he's even hoping that they'll get back together and be husband and wife.

Oh, man. I really don't want that to happen. I thought I did. But I don't. Not at all. Maybe that's why Mama doesn't write to him. She doesn't want him to hope for that while he's in here.

"I'm serious. You're looking great, girl," Dad says.

She shakes her head. "I'm not a girl anymore. I gave that up a long while ago. I'm getting old, Reeve. That's for sure."

"Yeah, well, me, too."

He leans back in his chair and looks up at the tiny window. I take the phone again.

"Hey, Dad, I'm learning to sail a boat. Maybe I'll join the navy and go on a submarine."

"Yeah. The navy? That's a good idea. I should have done something like that. So ya think the navy's taking ten-year-olds?"

He smiles. I like to see that. I made him happy.

"Dad, how come you didn't ever write or call us?"
I ask.

He glances at Mama, not me. He shrugs and lifts
his eyebrows.

"I'm not much of a writer, I guess."

No one says anything.

"But maybe you could call once a week?"

"Yeah, I guess so. Sure."

"Tuesdays," I say. "I'll be there. Call every single
Tuesday."

"Oh, come on now, Junior. I don't know about
that."

Mama frowns and rubs her forehead as if she has a
headache. She snatches the receiver from me.

"You can never see anything from anyone else's
point of view, can you? You don't have to be a writer
to know that kids need to have a father. A real father!
This is your son. Your son! Do you hear me? And
'yeah, I guess so,' is the best you can do? That's the
best you can give him?"

I've never seen her so angry. Her voice is shaking
with rage.

"Come on, Rachel. Let's not get into this now," he
says. "Let's try to keep this pleasant."

"Pleasant? Since when is ten years in prison pleasant? No. We will get into this. You know why I didn't
want him to come here? It wasn't because of the
robbery. I didn't want him to have to find out how
little you care about him and Tasha. No child should

70

ever have to find that out. And you've spent all this time, all these years sitting in here—you got heat, a bunk, meals provided for you—feeling sorry for yourself, always thinking about what the state owes you, how you didn't have enough rights, how you need more, how you would have got off if you'd had a better lawyer. Instead of thinking about what you should be thinking about, which is how to make a good life for your kids from whatever it is you got, even if it's nothing, even if it's trash, you make a life for your kids the best you can. . . . They come first, Reeve. Aren't you ever going to learn that?"

She's crying, sobbing and sobbing, and puts her hand over her mouth. I'm staring at her. I don't know what to do. I feel so terrible, as if this is all my fault. I didn't know it could hurt my mama this much to come here. Man. Why did I do this to her?

Then my dad speaks. "I know that, Rachel. I think about them growing up without me. I know how important the kids are."

"You do? You do? Then show it! You have to face your problems, not run away from them!" she shouts at him through her tears.

She puts down the receiver and hugs me. "I'm so sorry, Junior. I didn't mean to do this to you. You finish up your time. I'll just wait here." She digs in her purse for a Kleenex.

She gets up and stands right behind me. Slowly I pick up the receiver. My dad's looking crushed, or maybe just empty. He's staring at the wall, but there's nothing on the wall to see. I thought he was so big when he came in. Now the orange shirt kind of swallows him up.

"Hey, Dad. Think I'll grow up to be as tall as you?" I ask.

He smiles. "I hope you'll be a whole lot taller. Hey, you know I'm innocent, right?"

I nod.

"I'm not an armed robber, okay? Black men get picked up by the police for just about anything—a parking meter violation, running a stop sign. Anything can turn into an arrest. So I had some priors. Half the black men in this country got priors, Reeve."

I nod again, remembering the terrible moment up at the soccer field with Darnell.

"I was just getting my life together, cutting back on the alcohol, getting to work on time. And then I had that one bad night. But I'm innocent of the charges, Reeve. I don't want you thinking your father is a criminal, because I'm not. I didn't have a good lawyer, that was the whole problem. You gotta have a good lawyer if you want justice in this country."

Behind me, Mama snorts. She grabs the phone. "So you're innocent?"

"Come on, Rachel. I want him to respect me."

"Oh, really? What were you, a married man with one child and another one coming and a job, doing at two o'clock in the morning, sitting in a parking lot in a car loaded with guns and ammunition one block from a robbery? I raised these kids, Reeve. I raised them to be decent, honest, and respectful. Come on, Junior. Let's go." She taps on the door window with a coin to attract the guard's attention.

I pick up the phone. "Bye, Dad. I'll write you."

"Yeah? Maybe you shouldn't bother."

He sits, staring at the wall, holding the receiver, slapping it against the palm of his hand. It seems he's already forgotten about me. Mama grabs my hand and pulls me to her. As soon as the guard opens the door, she hurries me toward the exit.

Eleven

The long ride home is very, very quiet, and I fall asleep in the backseat, I feel so tired. When I wake up, we're just getting to Robin Lane. I have that confused what-day-is-it feeling at first. Then I remember my dad and the prison. I wonder if Mama's right in worrying that I will somehow turn into him.

In the driveway, in the front seat, Walter gives Mama a hug and strokes her back. I watch how gentle he is, taking care of her. He sure likes her. And that makes me feel a little better. Suddenly I want him to hug me, too.

"I don't think I'll come in right now," Walter says. "I'll call you a little later, okay?" He brushes the hair back off her face.

Mama smiles at him in a lazy way because she's tired. "Thanks, Walter. You're a peach."

He smiles and touches her cheek. "So are you."

"Sometimes, but not today." Mama laughs and opens the door.

"Come on, sleepyhead," she says to me.

Walter turns his head, "Bye, Reeve."

I lay my cheek on his arm for a split second before I slip out of the car.

We don't eat much for supper. Tasha's sleeping over at Ruthie's, and the apartment seems empty without her and Walter. Mama sits down to watch the evening news. She pats the sofa next to her. I sit close and snuggle up against her, and she spreads the brightly colored afghan over both of us.

"I'm sorry about today, Junior. I'm sorry I lost my temper. I shouldn't have. That wasn't fair to you at all, and I know that. I want to make sure you know I still understand how important seeing your dad is to you. And I'll back you up whatever you decide, I promise. You want to write him, I'll buy stamps. You want to call him, I'll pay for the call. Writing letters is good. It gives people time to think."

"But, Mama, is Dad guilty or innocent?"

"I don't know. I really don't. I only know what you know. But I've never seen a man arrested for sitting home playing blocks with his kids. Have you?"

We both laugh.

"You know what I like about Walter?" she says. "I like how patient he is. He's got nowhere else special to go. He tells me he's got all the time in the world. I like that."

I have to frown. "That doesn't sound too exciting to me."

Mama laughs. "Probably not."

But in a way I know what she means. My dad is so impatient. He can't even listen. So maybe writing letters will work better than phone calls.

After the news, I scout around for my sailing magazines and colored pencils. Mama turns on the radio and finds her New York City blues station. She takes off the stove burners and starts scouring them, singing a little to herself.

"I'm going to draw Dad a picture."

"Yeah? That's a good idea."

And so I set myself up at the table and get to work on a drawing of me sailing.

I definitely have to become a seaman. Now that I've seen the jail—I mean the prison—I know I am *never* going to be put in one of those places. I'm going to be a sea captain. Big and strong like my dad, but patient and steady like Walter and Ron. Captain Reeve McClain, Jr., at your service.

Later, around eight, there's a knock on the door. I rush to open it. It's Harriet, and she's brought Robert with her.

"Hi, Harriet. Hey, Robert! Come on in, you guys."

I pull Robert by the arm into my bedroom and close the door, while Mama and Harriet settle down on the sofa for a big talk.

"So. You went to the prison today?" Robert asks.

"Yeah. Oh, man, it was such a scary place. There were big towers with guards holding rifles. And barbed wire all over the tops of the walls."

"How about inside?"

"Ugly. Every door is locked. Hardly any windows. No pictures or decorations. Nothing. And it smelled like cleaning powder or something. Man."

"But what about your father? You saw him, right?" Robert asks.

Suddenly, I feel quiet. "Yeah. He and my mom got into a big fight."

"You're kidding. How come?"

"I don't know." I don't feel like telling him what Mama said in there. It's so hard to explain what happened.

"You gotta tell me, Junebug."

"I asked could he call me and Tasha every Tuesday, and he said he didn't know. And then Mama got really mad and ripped into him. About being irresponsible . . ."

I don't want to mention the part where Mama said he didn't care enough about us. I shake my head. "Anyway, my dad said he didn't do any robbery or anything. He said he's innocent."

"I bet he is, then," Robert says.

"You don't know!" I say.

"Doesn't matter. You have to be loyal to him. That's what counts."

I look at him, puzzled. That sounds screwy to me, but I don't want to start arguing. Not today.

"Hey, you have any snacks?" Robert asks.

"Are you hungry?"

"Yeah. Let's go out in the kitchen."

"Okay."

We cross the living room, where Mama is telling Harriet every detail about what happened. I open the fridge, and Robert spots some leftover spaghetti in a plastic container. He pops it in the microwave for two minutes to warm it up, while I pour a big glass of milk for him.

"You want some spaghetti, too?" he asks as he sits down to eat.

"No, thanks. I ate already. Hey, Robert, didn't you have any supper?"

"No." He eats the spaghetti in record time, then starts on the milk.

"Better be ready, Junebug. My birthday's coming up."

"Oh, yeah. When is it again?"

"November nineteenth. You think you can come over for it?"

I shrug doubtfully, my heart sinking. Here we go

again. Now that we've seen my dad, I bet Mama clamps down on me harder than ever about where I go and who I'm with.

"You have to ask her, Junebug. We're blood brothers, right?"

"We're food-coloring brothers," I joke.

"Ask her," Robert says stubbornly.

"I will, I will. Just not today."

"All right, but don't forget."

Harriet pops her head into the kitchen. "Come on, boys. I'm taking Rachel to the mall. I'm going to let her pick out some sweet-smelling bath salts. She needs a treat."

"Now?" I ask.

"Why not? It's only eight-thirty."

I put Robert's dishes in the sink. We grab our jackets and hurry out to Harriet's beat-up old car.

Harriet parks near the food court because she wants to take Mama to a store called Bubble Lovely or something like that. We have to hurry a little because it's getting late. Mama and Harriet are racing along, with Robert and me trailing after.

We pass the food court and turn left down a long hall filled with stores. And then I see Trevor at the entrance to the sports equipment store, where they sell all kinds of sneakers. He's with some older kids, one with a bandanna wrapped around his head like a pirate. Another kid is wearing a black tank top to show off his bulging muscles. They're Rex guys, I can tell. I bet those kids are sixteen.

I don't want Robert to see them, so I quickly pull him into the comic book shop.

"What are we doing in here?" he asks.

"I want to look for something."

"What?"

"Uh . . . I want to see if they have any dinosaur comics." It's all I can think of after seeing the Rex guys.

"Junebug! Are you out of your mind? Now come on, before your mother gets mad. Let's go."

"No! Listen. Trevor's here with some older kids. I don't want my mother to see them. They're near the sneaker store. Please, Robert?"

"Okay, okay. I'll keep my head turned the other way so he doesn't see me."

We peer out from the comics store. Some Asian guys are coming over to Trevor and his friends, kind of swaggering up to them. I think they're members of another gang. Just then I see two mall security guards start to walk over to the group. Now's our chance, while they are distracted. "Come on!"

Robert and I hurry after Mama and Harriet into the bath store. We stay near the entrance while Mama and Harriet wander around. It's kind of embarrassing in there. All women. Most of 'em old. Little round tables hold pink candles. Baskets of bath oil. Ribbons, flowery smells, funny-shaped soaps.

"Boy. I sure hope the guards made them leave. I

don't want Trevor to see me in here," Robert whispers. "I'd never hear the end of it."

"Yeah. No kidding."

Harriet buys Mama some bath salts and cologne. In the car Robert tells me that his mom has cologne and that it's also called toilet water. That starts us giggling, and I can't stop. I giggle all the way home.

"What on earth is wrong with those two?" Harriet asks.

"They're always like this," Mama says. "Two peas in a pod."

Two more elderly patients for Mama to take care of move into the apartments, making a total of six. These ladies, Mrs. Oliver and Mrs. Russell, have a lot of friends who drive them places, so they aren't around very much, and they don't take that much medicine. Mama can do their charts in no time. The first four patients are a lot more trouble.

It's a couple of weeks since we saw my dad, and he's called us twice. Tasha sent him a couple of Magic Marker drawings. I sent my sailing picture. Dad said he needed the pictures so he could hang them on the wall in the cell.

But then the nights come when Dad doesn't call. Two more weeks go by, and now it's the middle of November. At first I get worried that maybe he's sick, because he can't be busy. But then I slowly realize that Tasha and I have slipped his mind, that he's used to not thinking about us. And I realize that I'd better stop thinking about him quite so much.

Somehow I never get around to mentioning Robert's birthday to Mama. I don't make any plans for it at all.

Twelve

That rainy Saturday in mid-November, just before Robert's birthday, Mrs. Johnson isn't feeling well. Mama had to go down to her apartment in the middle of the night. Mrs. Johnson says she has indigestion. She's always getting gas pains. Early in the morning, Mama is up again, looking at her chart. She calls the nursing home director for a consult. Mama's looking pretty worried. Mrs. Johnson isn't getting any better.

Mama's on the phone a few more times with different doctors and people at the nursing home. Then she's on her way back to Mrs. Johnson's room. Just as she's leaving, the phone rings. Mama answers quickly, thinking it's the doctor. But it's not.

"It's for you, Junebug. It's Robert. Don't stay on the phone long, all right? I have a call in to the doctor at the hospital."

Robert. Uh-oh. I think I know what he wants. I pick up the phone.

"Hey, it's me, Robert! My birthday's next week. Want to go to the food court at the mall to celebrate? We can take the bus over."

"The mall? Really?" At least it's not at Auburn Street, so maybe I can go.

"Yeah. Just to hang around. After the food court, we can play games in the arcade. Stuff like that. Come on. It'll be fun! Besides, it's for my birthday. You gotta be nice to me."

"Let me ask."

It's great to hear Robert's voice on such a boring day! "Mama, can I go with Robert to the mall for his birthday?"

She's reading Mrs. Johnson's chart. She doesn't look up.

"Mama!"

"What? Can't you see I'm really busy right now?" she says sharply.

"I know, but I have a question. Can I go to the mall with Robert? It's for his birthday."

"The mall? How would you get there?" she says, barely listening, tapping her front teeth with a pencil.

"The bus."

"I guess so. Now get off the phone quickly, do you hear me?"

Then she says to herself, "I'm not waiting any

longer for the doctor to call back. I just don't like the way things are happening. I'm calling the ambulance."

"Hey, Robert, I can come!"

"Okay. I'll take the bus over to your house, and we can go from there. That way your mom can't change her mind."

"Sure. I guess. I have to get off the phone, Robert."

"Now quick! Give me the phone," Mama says.

She dials 911 and gives them the address, then hurries back to Mrs. Johnson's room. This time I follow her to see what's going on.

Mrs. Johnson is slumped in her chair. She sure looks bad. Mama and I move her to the floor. Mama puts a pillow under her feet and loosens her clothing. Then she rubs her face and calls out her name. "Belinda! Come on, now. Stay alert." Mrs. Johnson's eyes flicker open. "That's good. Don't drift off on us, okay? You're going to be fine."

Mama puts her stethoscope on Mrs. Johnson's chest and listens.

"What is it, Mama?" I ask.

"I don't know why she has stomach pains. But I think she also has an arrhythmia. Her heart is beating irregularly. Mostly I think she's scared."

The rescue truck arrives and backs carefully up to our entrance, while two of the medics come inside and down the hall to Mrs. Johnson's room, carrying all their gear. They slide her onto a stretcher, put an oxygen mask on her, and hook her up to a heart monitor. Then one of them calls the hospital emergency room for advice.

I feel sorry she's so sick. All those times she wanted me to look at pictures of her grandchildren, I wasn't very nice about it. Like when she tried to show me her photo albums. I acted bored and squirmy.

I tug on one of the rescue men's arms. "Is she going to be all right?" I ask.

"Oh, sure, son. Your mom handled this situation just right. When we get to the hospital, there'll be a doctor waiting to take care of her. We'll get her stabilized and run some tests. Chances are good she'll be home in a day or two."

I stand at the door, watching. All the rescue people are gentle with her, and they don't even know her. One woman tucks the gray blanket under Mrs. Johnson's legs to keep them warmer. She sees me watching her and smiles. People helping each other, no matter what. Mama's job sure is important.

Once the ambulance is gone, Mama leans back against the sofa and gives me a tired little smile.

Thirteen

By the time Robert shows up at our door, Mama is in her room, taking a rest. She has a splitting headache. She says it's a tension headache left over from this morning.

"I'm going now!" I yell. I pull on my jacket. "Bye."

"Be back by five," she says.

I have no problem with that. Three hours at the mall is not my idea of fun. As I step out the front door, light drizzly rain hits my face. It's annoying.

"Is it just you and me going?" I ask Robert. There don't seem to be any other kids with him.

"Nope. Trevor and Angelique are waiting for us down at the corner."

Now, why didn't he tell me that earlier? I stop walking and glare at him. "Robert!" I yelp.

"What? Come on, Junebug. Don't be such a wimp.

I want to include all my friends for my birthday. Besides, Trevor and Angelique went to a lot of trouble to come get you."

"You know my mom would say no if she knew Trevor was going. What am I supposed to do, go back and tell her?"

"She already said yes, so just come on."

I stand there as if somebody had punched me hard in the chest. Now I see that Robert is not one person but two, and that the Robert who signed the blood brothers vow with me is not the same Robert who hangs out with Trevor. With me he acts one way, with Trevor another.

Trevor and I are sure to get in an argument over something. Maybe I should go back and tell Mama that Trevor's going to the mall with us. But I remember what happened this morning with Mrs. Johnson, and I know how tired Mama is. Besides, this *is* Robert's birthday celebration. How can I let him down?

And what can happen at the mall, anyway? There are security guards everywhere. When Trevor was hanging around the sports store last month, the security guards came right over and made those guys split up before anything ever happened.

Mama doesn't want me to go off alone with Trevor, but we won't be alone on the bus or at the mall. So I decide it's okay.

I zip up my slicker. I can see Angelique in a yellow

raincoat standing by the curb on Bellmore Avenue. Beside her, Trevor is wearing a Boston Bruins jacket. Robert's just in a sweatshirt.

"Come on. Run," he says. "I'm freezing."

We run down Robin Lane to Bellmore, splashing through the shallow puddles. When Trevor sees us coming, he puts his arm around Angelique's shoulders as if to say, She's mine.

That's crazy. Other people don't belong to you.

We reach the bus stop out of breath.

"So," Trevor says. "You decided you could hang out with some of your old friends from the projects. Got nothing else to do when it's raining, right?"

I can't tell if he's kidding or not. "How've you guys been doing?" I ask.

He shrugs. "The same. Nothing ever changes at Auburn Street, you know that."

"Some things change. My oldest sister got her license," Angelique says.

"Whoa!" yelps Robert. "Watch out! I'm excited."

"She drove me downtown, and I bought a CD. She's nice."

"You have a CD player?" I ask.

"My sister does."

"I have a CD player," Trevor says. "You can use mine anytime. What did you buy, anyway? I forget."

"Whitney Houston."

"Ugh! Forget it!"

"Hey," says Robert, "the bus. Let's go." He's jumping up and down, he's so cold and wet by this time.

As soon as we get to the mall, Robert starts heading for the food court. "We can split up later on if you want," he says, "but I gotta eat. My friend Toshi at the take-out bar said he'd give me a birthday lunch for me and some friends."

Trevor takes Angelique's hand, and we head for the food. I follow, feeling jealous. I wish she'd dump him. That day at the beach, she said she might, but she didn't.

The mall is extra-crowded on rainy days. There are a thousand girls pushing babies in strollers, and dads carrying kids up high on their shoulders. We walk real slow behind three strollers in a row. It's like being in a traffic jam. If you try to pass in the outside lane, you get stuck behind the big potted fig trees they have all over the place.

I stop to watch the spray-paint T-shirt guy and nearly lose my friends altogether. Then I get jammed up against the window of an earring store for a minute. I'd like to buy Angelique a pair of earrings. I start to daydream about giving them to her in a little white box.

"Junebug!"

Robert grabs my arm. "We've been looking all over for you. Come on."

When we get to the food court, we see differ-ent kinds of food from all over the world: Japanese, Mexican, Italian, health foods, a French bakery—you name it—plus American stuff like hamburgers and huge chocolate chip cookies. Trevor and An-gelique grab us a table while Robert and I get the food.

"I'm getting two extra-large servings of chicken teriyaki, and we can split it, okay? You get the four sodas," Robert says.

"How often do you eat here?" I ask.

"I come here sometimes on weekends. At nine they stop cooking and start giving away the leftovers. A lot of people come in for free dinners. Hey, I need to do a lot of eating if I'm going to be six foot eight. These guys know me. Watch this.

"Toshi! Hi! It's me, Robert."

He turns into cheerful Robert, the one with the good manners, the one who's funny. The one who comes to my house to play. That Robert comes here to eat.

"We have a very good lunch for you today, sir. Hey, give Robert and his buddy extra-extra-larges on the teriyaki!" Toshi calls out.

Robert slides the trays down the counter. Toshi's wearing a tall red chef's hat over his long black hair, which is pulled into a ponytail.

"This is my friend Junebug, Toshi."

"Junebug?" Toshi asks, reaching out to shake my hand.

"My real name's Reeve."

"Nice to meet you. Robert, you come back after nine tonight, you can have whatever's left."

Robert is smiling as he carries the tray heaped with food to the table. It's a tight squeeze, making our way to the center row, where Trevor and Angelique are sitting.

"Hey!" says Trevor. "No cookies? Where's the dessert?"

"This is better for you. Low fat. Check out the bean sprouts."

"They look like worms!" Trevor yells.

Robert doesn't care. He's hungry.

The chicken tastes pretty good. I'm a little nervous about the bean sprouts, too, but they're all right.

A guy wearing a green apron and holding a dustpan and broom sweeps up all around us. At the table next to us are three girls with a cell phone, calling every guy they know and then laughing hysterically and hanging up.

Angelique is staring at the opticians' store, Eye World. "Let's go try on some of those huge sunglasses," she suggests.

"No way!" Trevor says. "We're going to the arcade. I told you that already."

"If we do something you want, then we should do something I want, too."

Trevor just laughs. "I don't think so. You can play games in the arcade. It's not like it's boring."

Angelique folds her arms and turns away. She looks sad.

Fourteen

"Ooof." Robert groans and pushes his plate away. He leans back in his chair, patting his stomach. "I think I ate too much. I feel like a hippopotamus."

"Yeah? Well, you look like one, too," Trevor says, getting up. "Ha, ha."

He grabs Robert's head in the crook of his arm and gives the top of it a knuckle rub. Then he walks off. "Come on, my man," he says. "Follow me."

"Hey, wait up," says Robert. "We have to clean our trays off the table."

Trevor looks back at us. "No way! What do you think they got food workers for? That sweeper guy will clean it up."

Robert shakes his head in disgust. So Robert, Angelique, and I clear the table off to Robert's satisfaction. Then we head for the arcade. It's the last store in the mall, across from the rest rooms and the security office. And it's crowded. It's always crowded.

Walking into the arcade is like walking into a wall of noise. Guys of all ages are in there playing the machines. A lot of the older ones are wearing camouflage clothes and combat boots and have shaved heads. Trevor's already on the prowl, looking for an empty game.

Right by the door are two large-screen racing car videos, where you feel as if you're really driving a car at 120 miles per hour. You have to drive without crashing or spinning out. Against the back wall is an old row of beat-up Skee-Ball lanes that nobody's using. Every other game is a fighter game with loud sound effects: shrieks, crashes, grunts, roars. And rap music is making a deafening thud, thud, thud in the background. Angelique puts her hands over her ears.

We walk around, checking out all the games. There's a line of three or four guys waiting for each of them—Immortal Kombat, Marvel Superheroes, Deadly Force, Ancient Kung Fu, real police stakeouts. In those, you don't shoot cartoon figures; you shoot real people on real live police videos.

A scary-looking white guy's standing in front of one of the police games with his legs spread apart, two hands holding the gun at arm's length, picking people off one at a time. Half of his head is shaved, and he has a Nazi sign, a swastika, drawn in black Magic Marker on the back of his denim jacket. Even Trevor doesn't go near him.

Trevor decides to wait for the large-screen Ancient

Kung Fu game. The guy playing it turns and says, "You're wasting your time, kid. I'm gonna be here awhile."

So Angelique and I wander over to play Skee-Ball. There's no wait at all, and you can't help but win tickets, it's so easy. Before ten minutes are up, we have enough tickets to go to the prize booth. I give Angelique my tickets so she'll have more, and she picks out a little yellow lion that you can clip onto a zipper pull.

"It matches my raincoat," she says, smiling and hooking it to her zipper.

"You know, I would have gone to try on glasses with you," I tell her.

"You would?"

"Yeah. Sure. So you like Whitney Houston?" I ask.

"I have all her albums. Her sound tracks. Posters. Yeah, you could say I like her." She laughs.

"Didn't she get divorced or something?" I ask. "I don't remember."

"Hey!" yells Trevor. "Angelique!"

Angelique jumps, startled. She looks at Trevor.

"It's my turn now. Come on over and watch," he says.

For what seems like half an hour, Trevor works the controls of the Kung Fu guys frantically.

Bap, bap, poof. Whompf. Bapbapbap. Thud. Unhh! Bapbap. Ki-yah!

The rest of us stand around, not saying much.

96

Twice the arcade manager comes over to tell Trevor his time is up, but Trevor ignores him.

Suddenly I see three older Asian guys, maybe fifteen or sixteen years old, come into the arcade. I think they're the ones Robert and I saw talking to Trevor last time. They're all wearing T-shirts with the sleeves torn off and camouflage pants, and they look as if they've been lifting weights. They stand in the middle of the arcade, staring at Trevor. Someone must have told them he's here. Trevor ignores them.

Teenagers that old can't want anything from kids like me and Robert, can they? But somehow I know they do. My old familiar tingly-scared feeling starts low down in my backbone. I wish I could fade away. I wish I had never come here today.

One of the Asian guys, a wiry, thin one, goes over to Trevor and taps him on the shoulder. He says something I can't quite hear. I see him jerk his chin upward as if to ask Trevor to go with him. He keeps his hands in his pockets. The other two guys stand slightly behind him on either side, like bodyguards.

Trevor leaves the arcade game, acting as though he's going to walk away. The Asian guy steps in front of him and stares him down. Robert and I are frozen.

"I can't help you," Trevor says loudly. "Okay? I already explained that. What are you, stupid?"

The Asian guy says only one word: "Outside." He pulls on his nylon jacket.

"Fine. I'll go outside. I'm not afraid of you guys."

For the first time, the Asian guy looks at us. "Tell these kids to get lost."

"I'm not telling them anything," Trevor says. "Where I go, they go."

He must think we're his little mini-gang. The Asian guys laugh. By now, I'm scared to death. I feel like staying right where we are, but already Robert's going with Trevor.

"Please! Come on," Robert pleads with me in a desperate whisper. "I have to back Trevor up. You gotta hang with your buddies. You can't let him go down alone."

Go down?

"What's going on here, Robert?" I ask.

"It's money. The Rex owes these guys money."

"Well, too bad. I'm not going anywhere."

I stop walking at the outside door. But Robert and Angelique keep going, following Trevor as if he's got them on a leash. So I push through the back door, too.

As soon as I step outside, I hear yelling. They're standing in the cover of the tall shrubs surrounding the mall entrance.

For a moment, the Asian gang leader stops yelling, and no one speaks. We're all staring at one another. I know something bad is going to happen, but I feel as if I'm watching a car that's crashing in slow motion, or I'm stuck in a bad dream. I look at the three Asian guys. They act sleepy, their eyes half-closed and lazy.

"Trevor, come on. Let's get out of here," I say. But no one seems to hear me.

"Trevor!" I repeat.

Is this what my dad did? Did he follow somebody else into something stupid? I want to stop this from happening.

"What's going on?" I yell.

"You want to know? Okay. I know this guy, right?" the leader says, pointing to Trevor. "Yeah. Trevor here is with the Rex. And it so happens that I have a little financial problem with them right now."

"Too bad, but I don't know anything about it, so get out of here," Trevor says. "You punk piece of—" And then he calls the Asian guy a swear word.

"Hey, hold on, Trevor. Back off." Robert starts forward and says to the leader, "He's sorry, all right?"

As Robert moves to take Trevor's arm, the gang leader shoves Robert. He is surprisingly strong and pushes Robert out of the way, hard in the chest, so that Robert's head snaps back against the brick outside wall of the mall. Trevor steps sharply back against the wall, too. He and Robert are side by side.

The leader folds his arms and looks at all of us. He's grinning. "What are you doing? Babysitting for the afternoon?" he asks Trevor. Then he looks at me. His eyes go back to Robert. "Listen. I got a little brother at home about his age. Give me that kid's sneakers, and I'll let the payment go."

Robert's wearing new one-hundred-dollar Michael Jordan basketball sneakers. They're his favorite thing in the world. Trevor knows that. Immediately Robert stoops down to unlace his sneakers.

Trevor prods Robert with his shoe. "Stand up," he says softly. "We're not giving them anything."

In that tiny moment, I see with amazement that Trevor really and truly cares about Robert. And suddenly, I'm willing to help Trevor, too.

"Drop dead," Trevor says to the Asian gang leader. "Leave the kid alone."

The leader grabs Trevor's arm and in an instant flips him to the ground on his back.

Trevor gets up slowly, and then he's holding a small gun. He must have kept it in his belt, in back, under his jacket. He points it at the gang leader. He swallows hard. His hand is shaking, but it doesn't make any difference. We're standing so close that he can't miss, no matter what.

"Trevor, put that down!" I yell.

"Trevor, don't," Robert says in a panicky voice. "He can have my sneakers. I don't care. It's not worth it. Come on, Trev."

Trevor never takes his eyes off the Asian guy. The two of them are locked together in some sort of old worn-out movie, where the same things always happen. It doesn't matter who the Asian guy is. It doesn't matter who Trevor is. Everyone knows by now that the Asian guy is going to get shot.

Robert starts crying, struggling with his shoelaces with shaky fingers.

"Get out of here," Trevor says to the gang leader. "I swear to God, I'll—"

It happens all at once. With a snarl of anger, the Asian guy jumps forward at the gun, trying to knock it to the ground.

At the same time, Trevor yells, "I'll shoot!" The bang happens almost at that moment.

Instantly, the two other gang kids take off running. Their leader falls down on his knees, clutching high on his upper chest near his shoulder. He rolls to his side, moaning. There's blood on his hand, and blood is soaking into the ground. I kneel down next to him, not sure what to do.

"Oh, my God," Trevor whispers. "Oh, my God. I'm on probation." He stares at us for a split second, trying to think. His eyes are wild. "Listen, Robert— No. Robert, you come with me. Junebug, here!" He shoves the gun into my hand.

"Take the gun. Cover for me, Junebug. Lie for me. You're clean. You have no record. Your mom's got a job. The cops won't touch you, I promise. If you say you did it, we'll all get off. Okay? Come on, Robert. Run!"

What's Robert doing? Running away with Trevor? They whirl away. They're gone. The kid on the ground groans.

"I'll go call the police," Angelique says.

101

She disappears, and then I'm alone with the Asian kid in the drizzle. The kid is moaning and rocking his head back and forth from the pain.

"We're going to get you some help, okay?" I tell him, kneeling down in the wet bark chips. "I'm sorry it hurts," I say. "I'm really sorry."

I try to take his hand, but he closes his fingers into a fist. "Go to hell," he says through his tears. "Just go to hell."

I'm still kneeling there, holding the gun, staring at the kid, when the policemen come pushing through the door, running through the rain.

Fifteen

What happens next is a big confusing mess. The police call for an ambulance, and one policeman is helping the Asian kid, trying to stop the bleeding from his shoulder.

For a few moments, early on, I stand in the rain, watching. When the police pull up the boy's shirt, they find a concealed weapon, a machete in a leather sheath, and a plastic Baggie with some kind of drug in it. Meanwhile, the Asian kid is trying to tell them I didn't do it, that a different kid shot him, but no one seems to be listening.

And there I am, still holding the gun. I don't know what to do with it. Does someone take it from me and set it on the ground? I think that's what happens. Or I guess I do that at some point. Angelique is gone. I keep looking around for her, but she hasn't come back.

"What's your name?" the policeman asks.

"Junebug."

"Yeah? Junebug, huh? Where'd you get the gun?"

"I—I don't know. Someone gave it to me."

He gives a disgusted laugh and handcuffs me. And that's when I start to cry.

By now, a big crowd has gathered. Some other security guards are clearing a place for the ambulance.

Angelique can help me explain what happened, but I still don't see her. "Angelique!" I yell. Maybe she can't get through the crowd.

"Let's go!" the policeman says. Oh, my God. They're taking me away. Where? How will Mama find me?

Two policemen, one on each side, lead me to the cruiser and push me into the back. I twist around in the seat, still trying to find Angelique. There she is! She's standing on the curb. Raindrops streak across the window sideways as we drive away.

I can't think straight. Where is the gun now? What are the police going to do to me? Why did Robert leave with Trevor? Is the Asian kid going to die? Is Trevor a murderer?

In the car, I notice only little things. The car door has no handle. There is a grid made of flat blue metal strips between me and the policemen. I wonder if they're taking me home. No one speaks. I worry I might throw up.

Finally I ask in a little voice, "Where are we going?"

"To the police station."

"Is that where the jail is?"

"Oh, boy," the driver says. "We got ourselves a real live wire here. How old are you?"

"Ten."

"Jesus Christ. They get younger every day," the policeman says.

Are they going to question me? I don't know what to say. But Angelique will come. She'll tell the truth. I know she will. And my mom will come. And then I can go home.

Now it's five o'clock. I'm sitting in a small, dirty hallway in the New Haven police station, juvenile crime division. The handcuffs were too big, so finally one of the juvenile officers took them off.

I've been sitting out in the hall for two hours, crying most of the time. There is a water fountain next to me, but the push button is broken. I sure wish it worked.

I'm so scared and confused that, for a while, I don't pay attention to the other people around me, all waiting for the intake officer. Then the boy next to me—he's got a shaved head and low-riding saggy, baggy jeans and a purple tank top—turns to me. He's wearing ankle chains and handcuffs.

"Hey. My name is Jor-el. What'd you do, man?" he says.

"I didn't do anything. A kid got shot at the mall. I didn't do it, but—but they think— I mean, I told them—" I start to cry again.

He looks at me, squinting his eyes as though he's measuring me. He knows I didn't do any shooting.

"You're lying for a friend, aren't you? You're covering up for someone." He says it as if he thinks I'm crazy.

I nod, completely miserable. What if I get put in jail, even overnight? I couldn't bear it. I swear I'd run away.

"You're either a great kid or real dumb!" he says. "Let me tell you something. Lying to a cop is a bad idea. You know that?"

I look at him and shake my head. "It is?" I ask.

"Yeah. You better have a real good reason for lying. You go to school?"

"Yeah."

"You do your homework and mind the teacher?"

"Yeah."

"That's good, cause they count that. This your first time in here?"

"Yeah."

"They count that, too. Your parents got jobs?"

"Just my mom. She does."

"Do you have a lawyer?"

I stare at him. "For what?"

"Ah, forget it. You don't need one. They're gonna

let you off. You'll be going home tonight. Don't worry about it. But stop crying, okay? It's annoying."

I manage to smile a little.

"There," he says. "That's better."

"What are you here for?" I ask.

"I stole a car," he says. "I do it a lot. It's easy."

He looks like he's about thirteen. "Plus I don't ever go to school. And I vandalized some stuff. Broke store windows." He shrugs. "I'm what they call a chronic offender. When I go in for intake, I act real polite. It helps. Hey, I got an idea!" he says, smiling. "Would you lie for me, too, as long as you're doing some lying in there?"

Then he says, "Forget it," and punches me softly on the arm, raising his handcuffs to do it. "Man," he says, "you look so scared. How old are you? About ten or eleven?"

I nod. Then finally I see Mama come in through the glass doors, looking for me. I jump up and run for her and throw my arms tight around her waist. "Mama!"

Sixteen

"There is no way my son fired that gun!" my mother tells the juvenile intake officer for the tenth time.

We're in a little office painted toothpaste green that barely has room for a desk and three wooden chairs. We're talking to C. Rodriguez. That's what his name badge says. There are stacks of papers piled high all over his desk, and piles on the floor, too. Worse than a teacher in June. He's filling out papers on me now, name, address, all that stuff. He looks up when Mama says that.

"I hate to tell you this, ma'am, but I hear that all the time. Cases like this are a dime a dozen. Every mother who walks through that door says the same exact thing: My son didn't do it. But in this case, we have two arresting officers who saw him holding the gun. His fingerprints are on it."

"Maybe he just picked it up off the ground."

"Now, why would he do that?" he asks. The officer puts down his pen and folds his arms.

"He's a child, ten years old. I don't care what you say, my ten-year-old does not have a gun. Are there other fingerprints on the gun besides his?"

"Yes, but they're badly smeared. We can't read them. Besides, he says himself that he did it."

"I said that once," I explain to Mama. "When I first got here."

"Junior!" she gasps. "Why? Why did you say that?"

"I don't know," I mumble miserably. "It seemed like everybody wanted me to. I thought if I said that, then I could go home."

"Everybody wanted you to? Who is everybody?"

"I don't know," I mumble again.

Maybe I did do it. By now, I am starting to believe almost anything. Maybe I really did. How did it happen? everyone kept asking me. Mrs. Johnson was sick, and it was raining. There was no one to play with. Mama was busy. Robert called, and I wanted to make him happy. That was pretty much it.

He's such a good kid. I love Robert. I really do, and there's no one else to love him. If I had to pick out a brother, I'd pick Robert every time. I wish we could adopt him or something. And now, if I tell the truth, Robert will be in trouble with the police, too, maybe even with Trevor's gang.

So how can I tell on Trevor without hurting Robert? I want to help those guys as best I can. I don't want to be the one to get them in trouble.

My head aches, and my nose and eyes are swollen from crying.

"But don't you want to find out the truth?" Mama's asking the officer. "Are you going to just let this whole case go without an investigation if my son pleads guilty?"

"That's right. Let's face reality, Mrs. McClain. The courts are jammed with assault cases. It would take years to process them all. First offenses like this, we can't take the time to chase them down. If your son pleads guilty to this assault charge, we can get him into some counseling maybe, or community service work. The odds are fifty-fifty that he won't do this again. That's the percentage of kids that learn from their first brush with the law. Reeve's young, he's got you, he's conscientious at school. He feels remorse for what happened. Keep him in school, Mrs. Mc-Clain. That's what we all want to see."

"Are you sure there was no one else with you at the mall?" she asks me. "Just Robert, right?"

"Robert? Wait a minute. Hold on," Officer Rodriguez says. "You didn't tell us that, Reeve."

Uh-oh. I said the gang leader tried to take my sneakers. I didn't mention Robert.

"Let's see," the officer says. "There was a scuffle over some sneakers, some pushing and shoving. Your son took out a gun to protect himself. The older boy

110

tried to knock the gun from his hand, and Reeve shot him in the shoulder. That's it."

"I don't believe it," Mama says flatly. "For one thing, where did he get the gun? You do not have a gun, do you, Junior?"

I duck my head down instead of answering. "No," I mumble finally.

"And for another thing, look at my son's sneakers. Worn out, down-at-the-heel. Not worth a penny."

Officer Rodriguez looks at my sneakers and smiles in spite of himself.

Mama won't give up. She's like me and Tasha—we're all so stubborn.

"There were no other witnesses? What about Robert, Junior? Where did he go?"

"Ummm . . . He got scared," I say.

"Robert, huh?" says Officer Rodriguez.

With a sigh, he flips back to the first page of his notes. He puts his hand to his forehead and reads the page over. Then he reads it again.

"Huh," he says. "Well, you're right, Mrs. McClain. There is some confusion here. The boy who was shot indicated that there was another child who actually did the shooting. We'll have to question everybody again."

The officer turns to me. "It's a possibility that maybe Reeve's covering for his friend. Sometimes kids do that. They think they're helping each other that way."

111

He takes my statement and tears it down the middle, then drops it in the trash can. He folds his arms and leans way forward, staring at me hard. "That statement doesn't hold water. You, young man, are a liar."

Mama looks at me sharply. I feel myself flush, and I stare at the floor.

"Well?" Officer Rodriguez asks. "Ready to tell me the truth? Where did you get that gun? Did you buy it?"

"No."

He sighs. "Mrs. McClain, this is something I'd like your son's cooperation on—details on where he got the gun. Let's try again. Tell me where you got the gun, Reeve."

"Why don't you answer him?" Mama says, sounding annoyed.

I can't.

Mama turns to face me. She takes my hands and holds them. "Junior, I know you did not buy that gun. You are not telling us the truth! You can't be," Mama says to me. "I didn't raise you to be like any street kid who doesn't know right from wrong. Did I?"

"No," I whisper.

"Reeve, tell me right now," she says in an angry voice. "Is it Robert's?"

"No." I want to go home so badly.

"Then whose is it?"

I shrug.

Mama is crying now. "I can't believe you're not telling the truth. I'm so disappointed in you," she whispers in a shaky voice.

Then I realize that it's my lies that are hurting her. She knows I'm lying, and she can't believe that I would do that. Suddenly, I can't either.

How is it that I came to choose doing what Trevor told me instead of what I know is right? I start to cry again. I can't bear to lie to Mama, but what should I do? I feel so confused.

Officer Rodriguez goes out and comes back with a paper cup of water. He gives it to me, and the cool liquid calms me down a little.

I have to think for a minute. I'm lying to help Robert, right? But how can lies ever help Robert? Even if they can, it's only for a minute, until the next time something goes wrong. I lean forward and put my head in my hands.

Why can't someone help Robert and Trevor? Why can't there be a rescue squad for kids? Someone to cook Robert supper. Someone to play games with Trevor. He likes games. He likes kickball, as long as he wins.

"This is pointless. Let's go home," Mama says gently, rubbing my back. "I'll bring him back tomorrow, Officer."

"No, please. Hang on one more minute."

The policeman's looking at me more closely now,

as though he can see me thinking, as though he finally realizes he's looking at Reeve McClain and not one more crazy, messed-up kid who doesn't care who he hurts.

"Listen, Reeve, you can help us get guns away from kids. It's up to you. If you don't tell me where the gun came from, then another child your age will be able to get one, too, and some more kids will get hurt. Do you realize that it just as easily could have been you who was shot? Or Robert?"

I flinch, but I know he's right. Any one of us could have grabbed that gun and shot someone, killed someone even. I look at C. Rodriguez in his navy blue shirt with the fold-over pockets. I have to tell.

"It's not mine. Not Robert's, either," I tell Mama. "It's Trevor's."

"Trevor? Trevor was with you today?" Mama says in disbelief.

Officer Rodriguez says, "Now we're getting somewhere. Tell you what. That water tasted pretty good, huh? I'll go get you a soda, while you pull yourself together. And when I get back, you will take a big breath and tell me the whole story again from the top."

He leaves the room. Mama comes over to my chair and hugs me.

"Mama, are you mad at me?" I ask.

"No, sweetie. Just scared and worried. And glad you weren't hurt."

I lean against her. She hands me a Kleenex, and I give my nose a good honk.

"You make sure you tell the truth now, you hear me? No more lying."

I nod.

What will they do to Trevor? Will he have to go to the juvenile detention center? Or to a real jail with grownups? Maybe if I tell the truth, someone will try to help Trevor instead of punishing him and leaving him to gangs and guns. That's the worst punishment of all—telling kids like Robert and Trevor that they have no future, that there's no way out of the projects and they're dumb criminals and can't learn like other kids. That's a lie, and it's not told by me. It's told by grownups.

Seventeen

Officer Rodriguez brings me a can of root beer. I pop it open and take a big gulp.

"All right. Let's get this show on the road," he says.

"If I tell, another kid will get in trouble. I don't want to get anybody in trouble."

"Reeve, here's the thing. Your friends already *are* in trouble. Someone could have been killed today. If your friends are shooting guns and running from the law, well, that's what trouble means. And right now, unless you tell me what happened, *you're* in trouble."

I think this over. It feels as though right in the center of my chest, I just heard the truth. I nod.

"Okay. You grew up around here, right?" I ask.

He nods. "Yes."

"What street?"

"Junior," Mama says, worried that I'm going to get going on the kind of question binge that I'm famous for.

"Near the Hill."

"I know where that is. That's a bad neighborhood, right?" I say.

He smiles. "It certainly is."

"Did you see your friends doing this stuff when you were my age?"

"Yes," he says more quietly.

"And did you help them?" I ask.

Officer Rodriguez sighs as he thinks back. "At the time, no. I didn't know how to help them."

"I can't tell on my friend unless I know he's going to be safe. I want someone to help him. Can you get him a lawyer? The kid in the hall told me that if a kid is really in trouble, he needs a lawyer."

It hurts to call Trevor a friend, but I decide it's okay just this one time.

Officer Rodriguez smiles at me and shakes his head. "All right. I know someone, a lawyer at the public defender's, and we won't plea-bargain your friend. I can't promise anything except that I'll try to get him in for a real trial instead of a deal. Maybe that way we can get him into some rehab. But I have to tell you, rehab doesn't work for all kids. There are some kids that just aren't willing to break the chain of violence, Reeve. In the end, making good depends on how strong each kid is. I'm sorry if that seems harsh, but that's the way it goes."

Officer Rodriguez gets ready to write. I tell him that Trevor is a chronic offender like Jor-el out in the hall, and somebody better help him because Robert and I sure aren't doing a very good job. But as for where the gun came from, he'll have to ask Trevor because I really don't know.

The scary part is, now that I've told Officer Rodriguez the whole truth, I have to be a witness at Trevor's trial in juvenile court. Robert does, too. I'm so glad I didn't have to mention Angelique and get her involved.

Officer Rodriguez knows I'm scared. He tells me to bring a crowd of people along for support.

What if the Rex shows up at the trial? Will they go after me for turning in a gang member? Maybe I'm still young enough that they'll forget all about this. But if I was older, I know my life would be in danger for sure. And now I know right down to my toes why Mama made us move away from Auburn Street.

As soon as we get out in the lobby, Mama grabs my face in her two hands and kneels in front of me. "Oh, Junebug, don't ever scare me again like you did today. How could I have let you go to the mall? What was I thinking?" Then she hugs me tightly. "Come on. Let's go home."

She finds a pay phone and calls Walter to come get us. We wait for him outside in the mist. I hope and hope that Robert understands what I did just now. I know he won't at first.

After nearly half an hour, Walter pulls up in front

of us in his car instead of the pick-up truck. He leans across the seat and opens the door. Tasha's with him, but there's somebody else in front, too.

Robert!

"Look who I found all alone in his apartment," Walter says. "I thought he'd better spend the night with us."

We three kids get in back. But then Mama says she wants me up front because she was so scared. So I have to climb into the front seat, and it's not even that embarrassing to have Mama keep hugging me.

"I'm so glad you're safe," she says. "Wait. Stop the car, Walter."

She gets out onto the curb and opens the back door so she can hug Robert. "And you, too, Robert." Robert starts to cry and she rubs his back. "Don't worry," she tells him. "You won't be arrested. We'll take you to give a statement on Monday," Mama says.

To my surprise, Robert looks relieved. He nods and leans against my mother. She gives him a kiss.

After Walter drops us off, Robert and I turn on the TV. But Mama turns it right off. She leads us both to the sofa and has us sit down beside her.

Uh-oh. What now?

"I know you're tired. But there's one thing I want to ask you both. Did you boys know that Trevor had that gun?"

"Yeah, sort of," I say. "We knew for a long time. You can't be in that gang, the Rex, without one."

"If you knew this, why didn't you tell me, Junior?"

"I thought you knew. Everybody knows. Besides, a lot of kids have guns. So it's easy for them to threaten you and tell you to keep quiet. A lot of kids buy guns when they get beat up at school or somebody threatens them or says racist stuff."

"Did you know Trevor had it with him when you went to the mall?"

"No!" I say loudly.

"Robert?"

"I didn't know for sure."

Mama gets up and walks to the window. Then she sits down in the rocking chair and rocks for a few minutes.

"Reeve, why haven't we been talking about this?"

"I don't know." I want to say, Because you're busy and tired and you don't want to hear about gangs and Walter's always over, but I don't. That's probably not fair. The real reason is that this is just the way things are. I guess I'm used to it.

"Robert, are you in that gang, too? I want the truth now."

"Not yet. I'm thinking about it, though."

"Oh, my God. Why?" Mama is shocked.

Robert shrugs. "So I can have a family, I guess. I like to have people around. My mother doesn't bother to . . ."

120

"She doesn't bother to what?" Mama asks.

Robert won't answer. He shakes his head.

"I want you boys to sit here and think over what happened today and what you did wrong while I get dinner. No TV, you hear me?"

"Yes," we mumble.

After supper, Mama pours herself a big cup of coffee and sits back down at the table, staring into the cup when she's not sipping from it.

"So, Mama? Is Mrs. Johnson okay?" I ask after a while.

"Huh? Oh. She's going to be fine. She'll be back with us in a day or two. Better than ever."

"Great. I guess. I hope she doesn't start chasing me around with her photo albums again."

Hey! Finally my mom smiles!

A little later, Harriet comes over, and Walter does, too. Robert and I go to bed the same time Tasha does. Robert goes right to sleep, but I lie awake for what seems like hours, listening to the grownups talk in the living room. They're talking about Robert. And I'm afraid they're going to call Social Services and I'll never see him again.

During the night, I dream about being put in jail. I scream, "I didn't do it! I didn't do it!"

"Quiet," says the guard. "Or do you want to be on the chain gang?" And he holds up a big length of chain.

I wake up and sit bolt upright in bed, my heart pounding. I look at Robert, but he's sleeping soundly.

I make myself lie down. Think about boats, I tell myself. And the wide blue water. But I can't. I have to get up. I throw back the sheet and pad quietly into Mama's bedroom.

"Mama! Mama, wake up," I whisper.

Her eyes open. She glances at her clock. It's just after two a.m.

"I had a bad dream," I tell her.

She scoots over in the bed, and I lie down while she gently rubs my back.

"Robert won't go to jail, right?" I ask.

"No, sweetie. But he does have to make a statement to Officer Rodriguez."

"You won't send Robert away to foster care, will you?"

"No. Of course not. Is that what you're worrying about?"

"Yeah. Mama, Robert and I are blood brothers. We signed a vow."

"Now, you listen to me, Reeve Junior. We aren't going to do anything about Robert until we figure out a way to make his life better—not worse. I didn't want to tell you this yet, because things may not work out. But Walter and I, with a lot of help from Harriet, are working on a way to do that."

"Not foster care, right?"

"No, no. Something just between us. Maybe he

could go to Darnell's after school, visit with Walter on Saturdays, and come over here on Sundays. Harriet can make sure he has a good dinner weeknights. We'll figure it out."

"Really?"

"Nothing's final yet, Junior. But we're trying."

Trying's good enough for me. I feel Mama's hand rubbing long, slow circles on my back and around my shoulders. It feels good. And the next thing I know, it's morning.

Eighteen

A month later, on Monday morning, we all have to go to Trevor's trial as witnesses. The main witness is the Asian guy who got shot, the gang leader. But since he was carrying a concealed weapon and selling drugs, he won't be considered very reliable. I guess he's been to juvenile court more times than Trevor. Well, he is fifteen.

The trial takes place in a huge downtown courthouse building, facing the city green. Even though we must have driven past it a million times, I've never been inside. The front steps are wide and not tall enough, so you climb forever and don't seem to go anywhere. The hallways are huge and echoey and lined with narrow brown benches. The benches are filling up fast with teenagers and their families. A sad-looking guy pushes a wide broom up and down the hall. Guess he's rearranging the dust.

My family has all turned out—Tasha, Mama, Walter, Harriet, Miss Williams, Darnell. Reverend Ashford wanted to come, but Mama wouldn't let him because of his emphysema. Police are stationed all over the place. We wander up and down, looking for the right courtroom.

When we finally find it, Robert's already sitting outside the doors with his mother. They smile at us stiffly, and we sit down to wait on the narrow benches.

For a few minutes, Robert and I pretend we don't know each other. Then, when his mom starts fiddling around for something in her purse, Robert slides over next to me. We watch his mother write a few numbers on a slip of paper. Then she stands up. What's she doing?

She gives the paper to Robert. I can smell alcohol when she bends over.

"Here. You can use this telephone number if you need to reach me. Just don't show it to anybody else. I haven't got time to sit here all day. And when this is over, go straight home. You hear me?"

"Yes," says Robert in a low voice.

Then she straightens her skirt and heads for the front staircase and out the door.

Walter strolls over and sits down with us. "What's going on, Robert?" he asks.

"She doesn't want to go head-on with Trevor's

mother," Robert whispers. "His family's been after us not to show up today. If there's no witnesses, then Trevor can't be charged maybe. I don't know."

Darnell sits down next to him and stretches his legs way out in the hall. "Hey, guys."

"Don't you have school, Darnell?" Robert asks.

"Yeah, but I'm not going to let you guys down. I'm gonna be here for you."

"Uh-oh," Robert says in a low voice. "Look who's coming."

There's Trevor! My heart bounces as if it's on a trampoline. His mother is with him. Trevor's wearing a shirt with buttons and a necktie, but the first thing he does when he sees me and Robert is yank the tie off and shove it in his pocket.

Next his lawyer comes—a public defender, Walter says. She's a tall lady in a navy blue outfit, with narrow spiky heels that click, click along the hallway as she walks. She introduces herself to Trevor and his mom, then pulls them across the hall and starts giving them instructions. Trevor leans his head on the cement block wall. He looks as if he's going to cry.

His mother looks more and more angry with him. She raises her voice. "I really can't take much more of this! I really can't," his mom says loudly. "I want him in a group home someplace. I told the judge that last time, and they didn't do a thing about it."

My family gets quiet. Everyone looks down at the floor, trying to give them some privacy, I guess. But how bad is that! Having your mother say she doesn't want you, right out in front of everybody.

Somewhere down the hall, a baby is starting to fuss and holler.

Trevor and his lawyer are now talking to another woman. A district attorney. She's holding a huge stack of files, one for each kid out here in the hall. She opens the file on Trevor. It's a pretty thick one.

I hear some words pass between the lawyer and the D.A., not a whole conversation, but some scattered words that burn in my brain. Trevor stands apart, pretending not to hear. But of course he can.

"This kid is trouble—five priors, robbery with a knife, drug possession. He turns thirteen next week. Used two ten-year-olds to take the rap for him in the shooting. That's not going to go over well at all . . . Truancy . . . So? What do you think the judge will go for? Is he rehab material? . . . Violating probation. The kid has a gun while he's on probation! Let me look at the notes . . . Angry. Impulsive. Fearful. Chaos at home. No remorse. Willing to implicate others . . ."

Fearful. That's the word that stands out the most. Hey, I'm afraid, too, I want to shout at Trevor, but I don't carry a gun. I was afraid and angry when some kids beat me up at school last June—four on one. That was so unfair. But I didn't go after them and shoot them. I learned some tai chi to protect myself.

Trevor raises his head and looks straight at me. He

rolls his eyes as though he's saying, Can you believe this? He wanders across the hall.

"Hey, Robert. Hey, Junebug. Darnell," Trevor says.

"You're not mad at us?" I ask, amazed.

"Nah. Not now. I was at first." He sighs like an old man. "You didn't do anything. I know that. I've been in here five times already."

"Are you going to get in trouble with your gang?" I ask.

"No. Kids get busted all the time from the Rex. Everybody goes to court. Some kids get off, some kids don't. Besides, we can recruit new members from the detention center. Hey, if I get sent to the youth center, could you guys come visit me?"

"I could write to you," I say doubtfully. Robert elbows me and makes a face. He doesn't like to write.

"Yeah. That would be cool, getting some mail."

The lawyer sees us talking. She puts her arm around Trevor's shoulders and guides him away from us to an empty place on the bench. "Sit," she says. "Don't move until we get called."

Trevor looks around her body at me and makes a face.

"That kid never gives up," Darnell mutters.

Above our heads the loudspeaker crackles. "The People versus Trevor Johnson."

Trevor stands up. "This is it," he says.

"Put that necktie back on," his mother says.

"Nah," says Trevor. He tosses it into a trash can.

"Someone would think you wanted to get caught, the way you act," his mother says.

He shrugs. "Okay, let 'em think that." He walks ahead of her and sits in the front row with his lawyer.

Walter, Mama, Robert, and I all walk in together. Tasha and the others follow behind.

Nineteen

When the time comes that I have to get up and testify, my heart is pounding so hard I think maybe I'll have a heart attack. But I speak up loud and clear.

"I just want to remind you, young man, that you must be honest. For most questions, simply answer yes or no, all right?" the district attorney says. She's wearing those cut-off reading glasses perched on the very end of her nose. I'm worried they might fall off.

"Yes."

"All right. Is your name Reeve McClain?"

"Yes." This is pretty easy. I look at Mama, and she smiles at me.

"Now. On November sixteenth, you and your friends went to the Torey Hill Mall together. And you first went to the food area to eat Chinese food."

"Japanese," I say. "Japanese food."

"Then you went to the video arcade, where you

were approached by three Asian teenagers. There was a brief argument about money."

"That happened outside. In the bushes." I look at Trevor, who's sitting next to his lawyer. He's got his head down, and he's staring at his shoes.

"After the argument about money, there was a scuffle over a pair of sneakers that belonged to Robert. Who shot the teenager?"

"Huh? Oh. Trevor had a gun under his jacket. He shot the Asian kid in the scuffle. And then he and Robert ran away. And I waited for the police to come."

"Okay, Reeve. Thank you. You may step down."

"You mean I'm done?" I ask.

She smiles. "That's all."

I let out a huge sigh of relief. That was easy. I cross the courtroom and sit down next to Mama. Robert leans over and slaps me five. Then it's his turn.

I grin at Mama. By now I know what I'd do if I was in the wrong place at the wrong time. I would speak up, the way I did just now, in front of everybody. Lying for kids doesn't mean that you care about them. Caring about them means you take the trouble to make things turn out right.

No way I'll ever become a man like my dad. Reeve McClain, Jr., alias Captain McClain, just made that impossible.

Robert keeps his head down and mumbles his way through his answers.

Trevor is assigned to nine months at the state youth center. The judge leans forward across his tall desk and tries to drill his eyes into Trevor's skull. "Get this, Trevor, and get it now. Chances are running out for you. Your time at the youth center is your time to start life over again. The first thing you will do is make up all the schoolwork you missed in sixth grade, as well as your seventh-grade work. Don't let me ever see you in here again. Do you understand?"

Trevor nods.

"Court dismissed."

Trevor, his mom, and his lawyer have to go up to the judge's bench for a private discussion.

Meanwhile Walter, Darnell, and Harriet go over to Robert. Walter takes his hand and gives it a little shake.

I look at Walter with his arm around Robert's shoulders now, bending low and talking to him in a quiet voice. I can see from here how upset Robert is. No wonder. He thinks he sent his only friend from the projects to prison. And his mother went off and left him here alone.

I take Mama's hand. "You don't have to worry about me so much, Mama. No matter what, I won't do anything that's bad. I promise."

She smiles. "You mean Harriet was right, and I was wrong, trying to protect you?"

Whoa! I don't want to get back into that argument they had at the beach. "I just mean, if something bad comes up, I'll be okay. Really!"

"We'll see," she says. But she's smiling, as if maybe she's finally going to ease up on me.

Yeah!

We wander out into the hall, Mama and I and Darnell first, Robert, Harriet, and Walter trailing after. Tasha and Miss Williams have gone to search for the ladies' room.

Suddenly we can hear Trevor's mom yelling at the judge. "I don't care. Do you see that attitude? He doesn't care about anything. Now you see what I have to put up with. I cannot discipline him. You have to help me!"

Trevor's mom bursts into tears and comes storming out of the courtroom and rushes past us down the hall to the exit. Trevor stays in the courtroom with his lawyer and the judge. I guess she is going to give him up.

Later I go up to visit Reverend Ashford in his apartment. Just as I expected, he's seated in his recliner chair, watching the news on TV. I sit on his two-seater sofa.

"How'd it go, Junebug? I hear you handled it real well," he says.

"Yeah. You could say that." I smile.

I don't feel much like talking about it, though. I'm hoping we can get started on a different subject. "Walter's coming over soon," I say. "He's bringing Robert."

"Yeah? That's good. You have to have some friends around."

"You know my dad?" I say. "He hasn't called for weeks. I mean, he can't be that busy." I sigh.

"I'm sorry about that, son. I truly am."

"Yeah, well. What time is it?"

Reverend Ashford checks his pocket watch. "It's almost six-thirty."

I jump up. "I guess I'll wait for those guys outside. See ya. Enjoy your news show."

He snorts. "Humph. That'll be the day."

I grab my jacket and sit out on the front curb, waiting for Robert to show up. He and Walter better get here soon.

Suddenly, there they are. Walter pulls up in his truck. He gets out and slams the door. Robert climbs out his side, carrying his gym bag. Looks like he's spending the night. I guess Walter'll take him to school in the morning.

"Hey, Junebug," Robert says.

Walter gives me a little swat on the top of my head and goes inside to see Mama.

I take a peek in Robert's gym bag.

"What's this? You brought more marshmallows?"

"Yeah. Walter stopped at the store so I could buy

134 of it, though.

them. And I shall beat you again, I believe, at marsh-mallow football."

"Nope. This time, I'll beat you!"

Robert smiles as if he's the wisest guy in the world. "In your dreams, my friend. In your dreams."